Marna

The Water Carrier

A Novel by Mary Daniels

DEDICATION

To all Marnas everywhere,

And anyone else who cares –

Never Give Up!

Thank you to everyone who has helped and encouraged me to write this book.

Special thanks to my dear friend Nicky Rowe for proof reading and Benji Linden for all your support and advice.

Mary Daniels

Part One
The Days Of Innocence

Chapter One

    There are four water taps here at Dahagey; they are called North, South, East and West but I call them dirty. They are all right for washing but I had some friends who drank the water from these taps and they are now late. I prefer to walk for half a day to a spring I call Eden, I love it there; I love it so much and wish I could stay there. It has green grass around it and sometimes a stray cow will be feeding on the grass. I sit down and watch the cow chew the grass and I lie down on my belly and roll over and over and smell the sweet grass and I laugh. I am not really allowed to go to Eden, it is only because my friend Sammi lets me through a broken piece of fence when nobody is watching and I have to make sure that I am back in time for lunch. Sammi is one of 'the green people,' that is what we call them because they wear green clothes all of the time.

    My name is Marna; I think I am twelve years old. Marna means 'never give up.' I remember my Papa telling me that. I don't really remember my Mama; I just remember that when we had to run away Papa called her a liar and she couldn't come with us. I was so confused because Mama never told a lie and I was sad that she couldn't come with us. Papa never spoke to me about Mama; I overheard him talking to some of the other men with us saying that Mama was a liar-be-litty. Did that mean she was a little bit of a liar? I did not understand much of what happened at that time, only that Mama was left behind and I never saw her again and my old life was gone forever.

I have one brother called Dopo; he is a little bit younger than me but much bigger and stronger. I don't know where he and Papa are staying as males and females are separated here at Dahagey. Sammi says he will help me find them; he is my friend although he is one of the green people. I know I can trust him because he lets me through the fence and he could get into a lot of trouble if any of the green people in charge of him found out. When I see him I recall the questions I have prepared in my mind that I want to ask him but he normally just laughs and says –

"Now what's my pretty little lady been conjuring up this time? "

I think he is embarrassed because he doesn't have the answers. I wonder why he comes here to work every day; does he go home to a wife and children? If I had a nice home to go to I definitely wouldn't come to work here; I'd run as far away as possible. I guess he needs the money, I don't know. How I wish I knew where my Papa was, he always answered my questions, he seemed to know everything. I used to wonder what people did before money was invented. If you didn't have money you couldn't come to our circus and watch the magnificent Marna (that was me) – unless you sneaked under the canvas of the tent when no-one was looking. Here at Dahagey there is no money, everything is bartered so I guess everything has a price really, just in another way. In a way that means that there is more of a price on everything and everything has a value – even people it would seem.

I was supposed to be dazzling the crowds with oohs and ahhs as Marna, the Magnificent tightrope walker – not carrying endless containers of water, back and forth, back and forth. And yet here I was living in this dreary expanse of brown and grey – muddy if it had rained, dry, grey concrete if not and nothing to vary the monotony.   Dahagey was an enormous camp; it contained far more people than it was originally designed for. All you saw for as far as the eye could see were beige or khaki makeshift, canvas tents. There were four disgusting toilet blocks which I avoided as much as possible and either went behind a bush at Eden or used a bucket. I did have to go to the latrine block once a week though as that was where we were allocated to do our laundry – highly hygienic! O how I longed for this all to have been a horrible dream and to return to my former, innocent, wonderful, care free life.

CHAPTER 2

I loved our life on the road, Dopo had a natural knack with all the animals and dear, sweet Papa and Mama who I can barely remember - we were a team and everything flowed smoothly and just seemed to work. I pictured our happy, tranquil lives progressing in a steady, secure way for the rest of my life. How incredibly, childishly mistaken was I!

We stayed in each place for about a month. We all helped to erect our circus marquee; there were usually about four or five other people with us apart from our family, we were a very tight knit group. In the winter we would camp out and stay put in one place until the spring. I liked it when we did this as it meant I could rest and sometimes I made friends, but then it was sad to leave. I thought our big tent with the massive pole in the middle was great; I used to lie on my back under the huge canvas and imagine that the pole reached the sky and could touch the stars and I wondered what that would feel like.

Papa said I was double-jointed; he used to joke that Mama didn't eat enough bones when she was carrying me so my bones were made of rubber instead. To me I was just who I was and didn't think about it really. I loved climbing up the steps to the trapeze wire; I don't think fear was a word in my vocabulary. Everyone was my friend, from the tamest lion cub to the ferocious bear; it never crossed my mind that someone could be mean or nasty or not want to be nice to me. Papa did have a temper and I remember his roaring shout, I used to think-Papa's being a lion again, I had better keep out of his way!

All I lived for was the trapeze. I would wake up early in the morning, often having dreamt about being on the trapeze, doing some clever performance and hearing the crowd cheer and after breakfast and chores were completed I would run up the eighty steps to the top of the trapeze. I would look out into the empty tent, take a deep bow and say – Good evening ladies and gentlemen, sit comfortably for you are about to be amazed as Marna the Magnificent attempts to perform acts never before attempted. I would stretch my limbs and warm up and practise my moves ready for the evening's performance. Most of my art was taught by Zena; I do not think that was her real name but she called herself Princess Zena and told elaborate stories how she was snatched whilst in her crib in a Russian castle by wandering bandits who demanded more money than her family possessed so they brought her up as her own and showed her how to walk the tightrope. She had scars on her feet from where the bandits made the rope red hot to teach Zena how to move quickly along it and if she fell off there were starving, snarling dogs underneath the rope waiting to eat her up.

Mary Daniels

Whether her stories were true or not nobody knew but she told them with such passion that no one would dare to question their authenticity. She would constantly complain about the food she was given to eat and say that her royal blood wasn't the same as ours and her constitution was missing the delicate cuisine she was used to. Although Zena shouted when she spoke, I liked her, I always knew she was going to be the same every day and she was a good teacher. She used to call me 'little dreamer' and I liked that because I enjoyed my dreams and often was sad to wake up and realise that what I had been pleasantly dreaming about was just that – a dream.

Zena blamed her illness on her 'meagre diet' as she called it; I used to think she would be happier if she just ate more but suddenly her bones began to stick out and you could see that she was in a lot of pain. Now I understand it was cancer but we didn't know anything about things like that back then. One evening Zena didn't turn up for supper. Mama joked – so Zena has finally had enough of our food has she? And we all laughed – until she was nowhere to be seen at bedtime and nowhere to be seen the following morning either. At lunchtime Papa said he was going for a walk and when he came back he was quiet and at supper he said – Zena's gone. I didn't understand what that meant but I overheard him saying to Zak who mucked out the horses that she couldn't bear the pain anymore.

So I became the solo trapeze artiste, I am not sure about my age but I can only have been about eight at the most, I was tiny really but nothing fazed me, I wasn't daunted by the responsibility. We always had a huge net to catch me if I fell – which I did frequently - but I think my youth was on my side as the audience would just think – poor little thing, she does so well for her size. An adult would never have got away with so many mistakes! The only thing I missed was Zena and our double acts. I used to love it when we would stand on opposite sides of the wire, high up on the top of the steps, waving to the audience and then looking at each other; we knew each other so well that we were perfectly synchronised. We would leap across the wire, stand on one leg and dangle precariously underneath, perform cartwheels and handstands – and we loved it. I suppose Zena didn't want to become a burden for us and little did she know that in a short while she would have been left behind anyway like poor Mama.

CHAPTER 3

I constantly pestered Sammi with news of Papa and Dopo. He would tell me how he had sneaked out paperwork and scoured the endless lists for their names – putting himself in great danger as he would never forget to inform me. He made me feel like I owed him so much, that I had so much to be grateful to him for. Sometimes I wished that I could simply drink the dirty water and not go to Eden and have anything to do with Sammi but there is something inside each of us I believe that makes us want to live; yes that drive can be crushed but most people want to survive, however brutal the conditions.

I know Sammi was kind and went out of his way for me but sometimes when he looked at me I felt uncomfortable, I don't know why. As hard as life was at the camp I didn't want to be late like my friends who drank too much of the dirty water. Then one day, I shall never forget it, I was walking up to Sammi as usual; it was a blistering hot day and I was deliberately moving slowly to conserve my energy when I noticed Sammi had his head down. He usually smiled and waved as I approached, he had the type of mouth that looked like it had too many teeth in and I would notice him smile a long time before

I actually reached the fence where he was stationed. But on this particular morning I couldn't see his teeth and I wondered what was wrong. I came close to him and placed my water container on the ground. I waited for him to speak but he was silent.

"What is the matter Sammi?" I asked.

"Why are you sad?"

"I am sad because I fear that you are an orphan now; I heard yesterday evening that your Papa was in the infirmary and became late in the night, I am so sorry my little one."

I looked at him, partly with sadness but mainly with anger. This place, this awful place killed my dear, kind Papa. I could never love anyone with such an intense love as I had for Papa – and to be told about his death this way was worse than dreadful. Also why did Sammi never call me by my name? I wanted to scream at him – my name is Marna, not 'my little one,' not 'an orphan,' and certainly not 'little lady.'

But I said nothing and keeping my head down I picked up my water container, looked around to check the way was clear and hurried through the broken fence. What about Dopo? Was he well? Did he know about Papa? I would have to ask Sammi but it would have to wait. I needed to digest this information and I was cross with Sammi for telling me so abruptly.

I stayed at Eden for the longest time possible; when I returned Sammi was waiting for me which was unusual as he was normally somewhere else when I slipped back through the fence with the water.

"You okay?" he smiled at me. I put down my water container and reluctantly met his eyes.

"I know it's tough," he put his arm lightly round my shoulders.

Acknowledging my silence, he sighed and said gently-

"Your Papa is still here, he will always be with you but for now how about I take the place of your Papa? You know how special you are to me little one and I hate to see you upset. I will always look out for you, you know that don't you? I will always be here for you and I will even try and answer your questions."

At that final comment I couldn't help but smile- who wouldn't? Dear Sammi, he waited for me to come back from Eden. I lay on my mat that night and thought about it all. Sammi didn't have to do anything for me so why did he? There was only one logical answer and that was that he genuinely cared for me. He certainly wasn't gaining anything by putting himself on the line for me. What did it matter to him whether I had clean water or not? It didn't and since I had lost my friends to illness I had become reluctant to draw close to anyone here. It felt like we were all only a few days or a sickness away from death and as lonely as I was I didn't want to risk making another friend just to have them die on me so I decided to trust Sammi; he was strong and as long as he kept his job and was not moved somewhere else he would be the one person I could rely on. I thought about all the questions I would ask him now that he had promised to answer them! I turned over and drifted off to

Marna
sleep.

CHAPTER 4

I did not find it easy getting out of bed the following morning, my heart felt as heavy as a rock; like one of those huge boulders the men in green shirts use to keep the entrance gate shut. Every morning I woke up with a crippling dry mouth, it felt like two pieces of stale, dry bread had been pushed together, one at the top of my mouth and one at the bottom and it was impossible for me to swallow the bread because there was no moisture to soften it.

The heavy boulder did not seem to diminish as the endless days dragged on. I longed for someone to call me by my name – Marna, Marna. I wanted to scream, my name is Marna, did anybody know, let alone care? My name is not 'girl' or 'water girl' or 'hey you.' I yearned to hear my dear Papa's voice call softly to me with his gentle, deep voice which always sounded as if he was laughing – Marna, wake up Marna, I have a surprise for you and I might open my sleepy eyes to find a tiny puppy in his big, work worn hands or he would lead me by the hand to the kitchen table where he had lovingly laid out a breakfast feast for four; normally of an omelette and bread and it was delicious and he always put a small jar of flowers in front of Mama's and my place. Never did I perceive that these simple days would be put in the region of my mind called memories.

    Papa would make an effort on the days that he was in charge of domestic duties; these were the days that Mama wasn't well enough to get out of her bed. I do not really have a place in my memory for 'well Mama' as I was only a toddler when the terrible accident at the circus occurred. There had been a storm the night before – so Zena told me – and the next morning it was still windy and everyone hurried to check that all the animals were all safe. We loved our animals so much and cared for them like they were our family. I know some people accuse circuses of not being kind to their animals and forcing them to do tricks that were cruel but that was not the case with our circus and we actually had a vet who always travelled with us. Papa's family all had circuses; it was all he ever knew. It was not just his job, it was his life; he had been brought up surrounded by animals and looking after them was as natural to him as looking after himself or his family. He met Mama when she came to watch the circus with her family when he was just a young lad. I think she was instantly smitten by him and enjoyed watching him care for the animals so skilfully and lovingly. Mama's family were quite wealthy and they did not approve of her falling in love with a scruffy looking circus boy with no prospects of a better life. In the end Mama and Papa waited for a couple of years until they were older and still feeling as strongly towards each other they got married. Even if not with Mamas family's complete blessing it was with quite a large dowry, as I know it helped Papa out with expenses he needed to keep the circus going.

The animals were understandably agitated and shaken after the storm but they were not physically hurt. Everybody tried to calm them down as best they could as it was still windy outside and raining heavily. The men went to check that the marquee was not damaged. When they inspected it they found that not only were there a lot of rips in the canvas but that where the rain had softened the ground and the wind had shaken the poles the whole structure had become quite unstable.

From what I remember the few workers that we had with us were not able to work fast enough under the demanding conditions. My Mama came with the other women to try and help. The animals were kept in cages at the back of the marquee and as Mama went across from where the animals were to try and help save the tent a huge gust of wind blew up. The main pole gave way and the structure fell down towards the already frightened animals.

We had an elephant at that time named Suzie; she had a three month old calf. Suzie was in an enclosure with her baby. As the tent fell down, the main pole crashed into Suzie and her calf was squashed. Suzie ran out of the damaged enclosure just as Mama was hurrying across the ruined marquee, trying to get out of danger's way. Suzie reared up and attacked Mama.

This is why Mama didn't escape with us when the soldiers came and we had to say goodbye to our beloved circus. She could hardly walk after that, let alone run away. I still don't understand why Papa called her a liar when we were preparing to leave. He said she was a liar-bility and would not make it to the refugee camp. It was heart breaking having to leave her behind but I know papa was right. She would not be able to keep up with us but she never lied. One day I will ask Sammi what liar-bility means. I will wait until he is in a good mood but now I need to get up and fetch some water because I am not the only one with a dry mouth.

CHAPTER 5

We all suffer the same here, it doesn't matter if you were a doctor before or you went to the dump to salvage what you could in order to stop you starving; we are all in the same situation. Dahagey is not as big as some camps that I hear about, I think there are about two thousand people here on an area of ground not much bigger than where we held our circus shows. We only really hear news when there are new arrivals. Although this was practically a daily occurrence they don't always come into my area which is in between the north and east sections. I am grateful this is where I am as it is at least possible to occasionally find a little bit of shade to relieve the relentless burning sun.

I remember only too clearly the day Papa, Dopo and I arrived here; I think it must have been just over a year ago as I have witnessed all the four seasons. We queued for two days before we reached the front of the queue and could see the huge gates keeping us all in. I was trying to figure out what was happening to the people in front of us and as far as I could make out the women and children went to the right and the men went to the left hand side. But there were exceptions as I saw families with very small children staying together – how I wished that we had a small child. As the queue in front of us decreased I began to grow terrified at the thought of being separated from Papa and Dopo but I realised with a nagging certainty that there was absolutely nothing I could do about it. We had no choice; our enemy, the Konubo tribe had had some sort of dispute with my people and we were no longer allowed to live where we lived. That is the extent of my knowledge - one day we were going about our everyday lives, the next we were marched off our land at gunpoint. Of course we had heard rumours but we just thought they were stories that people had exaggerated and as Papa kept repeating as we walked for a week before we arrived here – there was no way of escaping our fate even if we had had any warning about how dire the situation truly was. As we were marched along at gunpoint that week we witnessed the most horrendous sights – whole villages wiped out, some burnt to the ground and there were bodies lying along the side of the roads and paths, often having been there for days. Papa kept saying sorry to me and Dopo – over and over. I suppose he didn't want us to witness such atrocities at so young and impressionable an age. I held his hand a bit tighter every time he apologised, trying hopefully to reassure him that none of this was his fault but as the week wore on I worried about his sanity as he would constantly mumble to himself and shake his head– dear Papa.

CHAPTER 6

So my fears became my reality and as Papa, Dopo and I approached the huge, imposing, metal gates so we were immediately and quite forcibly separated. Nobody wanted to witness any emotion shown in this faceless, inhuman prison. We were informed that Dahagey had been constructed for our own good because without it we would either die of starvation or be killed by the crazy intruders who had violently trespassed the land where we had lived peacefully for countless generations. Obviously I kept my mouth shut but I wanted to shout – in what universe is this awful existence for our good?

I was assigned a primitive, makeshift, canvas construction in the middle of a long line of identical faceless, khaki-coloured nine foot square spaces. My initial worry was how would I identify which tent was mine? I soon realised that staying opposite me I had a flamboyant, lively family known as the Rufaros and there appeared to be constant activity outside their tent so that worry quickly dissolved. There was a metal camp bed inside my tent with a thin mattress and blanket. I felt it was rather fortunate that I was used to camp life as although we had a beautiful caravan which was my childhood home Dopo and I often chose to sleep in a small tent we owned or even under the stars themselves.

    As the days went by I became increasingly despondent with the knowledge of never seeing Papa, Dopo and obviously Mama again. The strange thing was that I felt Dopo close to me and I had done for a while – but not Papa. Sometimes I felt as if Dopo was there with me and I could hear his voice inside of me but Papa seemed so far away I couldn't reach him. I was aware that my thoughts of Papa were consuming my life and that it was becoming an unhealthy obsession; I told myself this and I suppose with the lack of anything else to occupy my mind my thoughts ended up drifting into that singular, negative fixation. This continued in the same vein for several weeks until one night I had a dream. I dreamt that I was standing on one side of the high barbed wire fence that is here at Dahagey and over on the other side stood Papa. There were other people present but I could clearly recognise Papa. I called out to him but he had his head to the ground and appeared not to hear me – I screamed – " Papa, Papa, you must be able to hear me, look up; it's Marna, I am well, please look up. Please look up and let me see your face, please dear Papa." My voice was beginning to grow hoarse and the dream woke me up and I noticed my pillow was drenched with my tears. I determined after that to think no more about Papa but to continue surviving each day and living one day at a time, keeping my head down and not thinking too much about my future or what might be. I had known some people at Dahagey to literally go mad by thinking about their freedom – and lack of. I think that meditating upon life outside the camp just made the fencing draw in on you and make your encampment all the more unbearable.

Sammi tried his best to cheer me up and make my days less mundane. When we lived with the circus and after Mama became less able I almost solely took over the cooking and I found that not only did I enjoy cooking but that I was quite good at it. I thoroughly took pleasure in looking at the food we had available – which often wasn't very much at all – and then figuring out how to make a tasty meal out of those few ingredients. I often found that by simply adding a herb or spice it could make all the difference in making a flavoursome meal as opposed to a very bland one. I would go wandering about the countryside seeking various herbs and I taught myself rather a lot in those days. So when we arrived at Dahagey and after the shock of being separated from the men I thought – well at least I know how to cook and maybe I can help other people here too with my skills. But no, it was not to be, at this camp there was one canteen and you went there three times a day – early morning, just after sunrise and you were given a sweet mug of tea and a slice of bread and occasionally jam. Then lunch was served about 2 p.m. and normally this consisted of a disgusting, barely edible stew and then just before sunset, at about 8 p.m. you would be given another mug of tea and occasionally something to go with it.

I used to joke with Sammi when he ordered me back for lunch. I would say,

"Why do I need to come back for lunch? I think they are trying to kill us all with their food, do you want me to die?"

He would laugh and reply,

"I don't want you to die my little one, who would I have to worry about each day? You give me grey hairs when you take so long to fetch the water. Now go, hurry, and don't be late!"

I asked Sammi on several occasions whether he could ask on my behalf if I could help out in the canteen but he said I was too little and wouldn't be able to reach things or carry the heavy pans. I found this rather a peculiar excuse but I didn't want to say 'oh when I am older then?' The thought of staying here and doing this same routine day after day was just too unbearable to contemplate. Obviously I tried to ask the canteen workers myself but the problem there was language and Sammi said you have to be careful or they could turn nasty so just be grateful for what you are given; this is what he told me.

I learnt from other women who had been on other camps that this was not always the way the camps worked and that on some you did your own cooking. One woman informed me that there had been a serious fire at Dahagey a few years ago and that they had been thinking of installing a canteen anyway; partly because it was easier and also there had been some violence when people had been starving and were bartering for food. So it seemed a logical solution to install a canteen and have set meal times. It was actually quite nice to have some form of structure to the otherwise tedious drudgery that had become my existence.

On the odd occasion that we had visitors, people

would arrive in jeeps and they always seemed to have the same look about them. They always had their head tilted to one side and looked at us pitifully. Then a few days later some bags and crates of food would arrive and we would never see those rich people again. I used to imagine them going to bed in their high, soft beds saying to themselves – oh I am such a compassionate person, what a wonderful thing I have done. And they will give themselves a big pat on their back, turn over and sleep peacefully. But it didn't seem to matter what new food arrived because the so called cooks had no imagination regarding what to do with it, they never made anything different or interesting and nobody thought to bring us any salt. I always thought that salt was vital in the heat but then I soon realised that our well-being was not high on anyone's list of priorities.

There was a great deal of sickness at Dahagey, especially diarrhoea. The smell from the toilet blocks was horrendous; it was so bad that most people did not use them and would dig their own holes. I am not sure which was more hygienic; for me personally because I had my good friend Sammi I would find a bush at Eden and go there. Some days I would feel strangely free when I lingered at Eden; partly because I was on my own and fending for myself and that in itself was quite liberating and also because I had escaped the confines of Dahagey, even if only for a few short hours. I really feared becoming ill; it was one of my most common obsessive worries! If I was to die whilst in the camp I wanted it to be at night - and quick with no suffering.

On the whole everyone kept themselves to themselves and were so caught up with their individual thoughts or too traumatised having lost or been separated from loved ones that they did not have the energy to communicate or interact. This suited me fine, I quite enjoyed wandering around and doing my own thing, even when we queued to get our food nobody really spoke. Our tents were all lined up very close together. On one side of me were an elderly couple who I think had been there some time; every move they made was as if it was in slow motion and they even spoke slowly. They seemed sweet but they never really spoke to me or asked my name so I rarely spoke to them, we would nod our acknowledgement of each other. The Rufaros were the complete opposite. I never worked out the total amount of people who actually lived in the one tent but it was a lot. I think there were three generations altogether – grandparents, parents and numerous children. I think there were aunts and uncles there too; their family name was Rufaro and they were from the Konubo tribe. I had heard Papa speak of the name Konubo and I often heard it mentioned in the days before we were ordered to leave the circus and also as we marched on our way here. It was never spoken in a nice way but I liked having the Rufaro family as neighbours; they were kind to me. Every possession at Dahagey was valuable, if your mug got stolen for instance then you weren't given any tea or stew and if you did not have a blanket you would be cold at night because the nights were often chilly and could actually reach freezing point on some nights in the winter. I felt that with the Rufaros living opposite me it was safer somehow when I had to leave my tent because obviously there was a vulnerability to being a lone female on a camp like Dahagey. I would share my water with them and sometimes play in the dirt with the children. Their faces were always filthy but I loved to watch them play and smile and laugh. What a blessing it must be to be ignorant and innocent I thought to myself.

One day I woke up to hear the usual daily noises but on this particular day as well as the normal noises I heard the most awful cough coming from the Rufaro baby. I walked over to the canteen and had my tea and bread and on my return I stopped outside their tent. There were some children playing outside as there usually were but I just could not walk on having heard the child in so much distress. I poked my head in the door and found the mother frantic with worry, stroking the child's head with a cool, damp cloth. The mother was silently crying and shaking her head; I told her I would fetch some water – what else could I say? What else could I do? A doctor came to visit Dahagey once a week, it was always on a different day and there was no appointment system. I went to fetch the water feeling very sad, sometimes I wished I was tougher or maybe didn't have a heart at all; surely it would be better not to feel anything than to carry this amount of pain constantly?

CHAPTER 7

When I returned with the water and walked towards the Rufaro's tent there was only silence; I slowed down my pace and hesitated whether to approach their tent or not. If I did what would I say? I chose the relatively easy option and left the container of water outside their door. I could see heads bowed low in grief inside because even the most private of times here are public as the flimsy door consisted only of a canvas flap.

The nights were beginning to get colder and there was nothing about this forlorn place that was conducive to the falling night temperatures. One morning I meandered over to my usual broken piece of fence. From a distance I noticed Sammi smiling, holding something in his hands.

"Look what Sammi has for you today, my princess. I couldn't have you getting cold now, could I? I just so happened to walk past the building where they sort out the donated clothes. I stopped and thinking of you, as I often do, peered in and saw an array of soft, warm blankets and this colourful jumper. No more freezing nights for my precious, little water carrier."

Upon saying this last comment Sammi ruffled my hair. I know he meant well but it annoyed me when he did this. I really loved my new jumper, to feel the softness of the wool against my body was heavenly. It smelt lovely too and as I often did in these situations, I thought about the people who donate items to camps like ours. I imagined it must have been a young woman who sent this jumper as it had a low v neck in the front and a partially open back with two straps of material holding the knitted garment together across the back. It had a nice pattern on the front with a pink, peach and white design which was lovely but so impractical here. I thought about the young woman and I am sure that her intentions were good but if she could just live in my shoes for even a day she would witness the dust - the incredible dust that gets into everything, especially nice, soft wool. Also I couldn't help but feel disappointed and a little angry; if she could walk in my shoes/ bare feet around Dahagey she would experience a thousand eyes ogling at her from sleazy men who look at me as a potential target. I know this and I am not naïve, I am mature for my age and I am very aware of my developing breasts and how a man's mind thinks – that he wants to be the first to touch them. And the v neck only encourages their ever-present temptations.

I felt so grateful to have Sammi on my side; I know he looks at me too intently sometimes but as I got to know him I felt I could trust him. He was kind to me and there was nothing in it for him to go out of his way and collect a jumper and warm blanket for me; it was only because he cared. Every day there seemed to be more and more new people entering the camp and I don't think the donated items were distributed fairly at all; in fact the longer I stayed here the more corruption I noticed. So it would have been very likely that I would not have received anything had it not been for Sammi. Also at this time of year, in between summer and winter there was an increase in diseases and something simple can quickly develop into a serious problem without proper sanitation, medicine – and of course clean water of which I had Sammi to thank.

Sammi was of medium height and build and apart from his wide smile with luminous white teeth which seemed to light up his whole face there was nothing remarkable about him. I found it incomprehensible how Sammi was a respected, free man and other men who looked extremely similar to him were locked up here. How did someone recognise which tribe they were from? What made two men different? What gave one the right to be respected and earn a living whilst living at home and the other uprooted from all he knew and placed involuntary in this slum with very little hope of regaining his former life or anything closely resembling it? One of the main topics of conversation at Dahagey was about tribes and your family roots. I took the opportunity one day to ask Sammi why Dopo went to live with the men when he is at most eleven years old. Sammi said,

"Very few people arrive here with any documents and if they do the authorities do not trust that they are not forgeries so they allocate people on their height and appearance. If Dopo had been shorter and kicked up a fuss leaving his mother then he probably would have gone with the women and children; but sadly that was not the case was it? I am sorry little one but given the choice between going with you or his father he would choose his father, wouldn't he?"

Sammi was right and it made sense. There were a lot of rumours that were spread here at Dahagey. I didn't take any notice of most of them as most were wishful fantasies and I didn't believe it was possible to get away from here without the help of the authorities; and anyway where would you go? But on this occasion I kept hearing the same story with little variation; and this story was about some fighting in the men's section of Dahagey. Apparently some men had smuggled in some arms and knives and there had been two nights of rioting and looting of the supplies. The Rufaro family said it was because the men were cold and desperate. It was possible for the temperature to reach freezing at night here and the flimsy tents were scant protection and when the wind cut through the canvas. Whatever bedding and clothing we possessed seemed inadequate. There were so many things I did not understand here but I had a feeling that the fighting was something to do with some members of the Rufaro family.

I had befriended a young woman here called Kali – or that is what everyone seemed to call her. The name Kali means 'energetic' and I suspect that was her nickname. I liked Kali; she was a tiny ball of energy. She was also an enigma; she wasn't a refugee here but didn't wear the green uniform either. For some reason she was able to freely pass through both the male and female quarters; maybe she was a charity worker, I wasn't sure but I enjoyed watching her walking fast with a purpose as opposed to watching people with their heads down, trudging along aimlessly, just wishing the day to end and desperately hoping for a change. Her positivity was contagious; the first time I met her I thought to myself that this is a person who could maybe come in useful one day. I really made no effort with anybody else but with Kali I made a point of saying hello and stopping to speak with her when our paths crossed.

It was Kali who first notified me of the fighting that was going on in the men's quarters. I told her Dopo's name and she said she would do all she could to find out about him and would check the register, even from the infirmary. I couldn't really understand how she could appear so positive. How could such a huge complex such as Dahagey cope with so many names coming and going; especially as so many names were the same and so many people had no identity cards? I came to the conclusion that Kali definitely did not live at Dahagey; she would have understood the impossibility of trying to trace one individual. No, her vitality would have been zapped long ago.

Often at night I would lie in bed trying to sleep and ignore the cacophony of various noises going on around me. On such occasions your mind could very easily wander in all sorts of directions and you would ponder things which in daylight hours would seem absurd. On one particular night I had a flashback to a lunchtime when I came through the broken fence as was my norm. Only this time I noticed Sammi was standing a little way away from the fence but I know that he had seen me. What was different about this time was that he was not alone. I was running a bit late in order to be at the canteen time for lunch and I didn't take any notice of the situation at the time. Now as I lay in bed I suddenly remembered that Sammi was standing there laughing with a fellow green shirt. Hadn't Sammi made a big point to me about how dangerous it was for him to let me through his precious fence? Now here he was talking with his colleague who I am certain saw me creep through the gap – so where was the danger? Where is this great sacrifice that you are making for me Sammi? You know the one that I am supposed to be eternally grateful for?

It didn't make sense, life sure was complicated.

CHAPTER 8

The days dragged on becoming more and more repetitive as I became more and more morose. I was terribly lonely and worried that I might develop what was known at Dahagey as 'Rolex syndrome' because you could set your watch by how mundanely accurate a Rolex person's routine had become. After you had been in the camp awhile – and I had been there for over a year depressingly – you accustomed yourself to a habitual routine. You literally did the same thing at the same time day in and day out – no days were any different. I remember one day we were queuing up as usual for our regular lunch of soup and bread but the ovens were not working. This simple issue upset me for days – and then I became upset because I had allowed it to consume me. There was nothing else going on in my life. This is a picture of our institutionalised life; how different compared to my former life which was increasingly feeling alien to me, like that life belonged to someone else in a faraway land.

I vowed to myself that when this nightmare was eventually over I would never take for granted running barefoot over the dew covered grass first thing in the morning or enjoying a meal with family and friends, or sitting round a camp fire feeling safe and happy and loved. I couldn't decide whether it was better to remember those days or to forget them and just have them locked away in a secret compartment in my mind. However I looked at it I couldn't stop my dreams which were either wonderful memories of those colourful, fun filled, childhood days or were nightmares about never living in freedom again.

One of the things I found the hardest to cope with was the lack of company. I know that sounds strange as I was surrounded by people but there was nobody close to me or that I could truly trust. As much as I liked and respected Kali, I was never quite certain about her; I always wondered whether she had ulterior motives. I had had a lot of things stolen from my tent and it made me distrust everyone and question everything they said and every little look or gesture, however innocent it may actually have been. I think if you have no family with you, you can say what you like, there is no accountability. I know there were people here who lived in a constant fantasy world as it was a preferable option than their reality and that maybe just about kept their sanity. When you live in a situation where every decision is made for you your mind soon becomes mush.

I know I had Sammi but there was always that barrier – partly because he was a green shirt but there was also a nagging doubt inside me as to his true motivations in helping and befriending me. A few days after he had obtained the jumper for me I approached the fence as I normally did and we chatted for a bit. He told a couple of jokes because he said he wanted to see my pretty smile.

I noticed he kept looking at my breasts which were just starting to develop. He briefly brushed his hands over them and I felt very uncomfortable and ran off.

Subsequently I started talking to Mrs Rufaro. I would bring her round some water after I had had my lunch. I enjoyed sitting outside her tent with her, it was peaceful and the afternoons could seem quite intolerable with hour after hour of monotonous boredom. There were normally about four thick, woven, linen mats outside of the Rufaro's tent and it was the closest thing to feeling like a family, sitting there with these loving, warm people who always made me feel welcome. One of the female relatives- I was never quite sure of the exact connection - liked to braid my hair. Zena used to do it for me at the circus before she became late and I never really got the hang of doing it myself. This dear woman would quietly sit behind me and start braiding my hair and put the prettiest beads at the ends, it really cheered me up. I had started to take a nap in the afternoons and that had become another thing I beat myself up over because I certainly didn't need it even if my nights were disturbed by all the noise. I was young and should be in the prime of my youth and full of energy. I was only too aware that not only had my fitness levels dropped but I was nowhere near as flexible as I was when I was a trapeze artist. Taking a nap was a habit I needed to snap out of and by sitting outside my neighbour's tent was one sure way of staying awake.

Everyone called Mrs Rufaro 'Ummi' and so I started to call her that too. She was an over-sized, colourful woman with a contagious laugh which made her whole body wobble. I could even hear her laugh from my tent but she was a sensitive soul and even at my tender age I knew she has suffered greatly, not least having so recently lost her sweet baby boy. Ummi was an excellent listener and when I woke one morning to find my bed stained with menstrual blood it was Ummi who I turned to. She was so caring she made me cry – quite a feat as I rarely showed any emotion – and when I returned from fetching the water she had placed a pile of cut sheets, folded neatly by the side of my bed which she had kindly washed for me.

A strange phenomenon began to develop in the following weeks. I struggled to understand why certain people began to snub me and deliberately nudge me when I was queuing for food and once made me spill my soup. It was hot and it stung my chest as it splashed over me. I asked Sammi about it and he gave me his familiar look like he always did, as if to say – oh you are so naïve, don't you understand anything that goes on around here? No actually, I didn't, or very little anyway. He told me it was because the Rufaro family belonged to the Konubo tribe and that many people at Dahagey blamed them for killing their family members and burning their villages. Sammi said the camp authorities tried to keep the tribes separate but it was a difficult task as many people were scared and lied about who they were. I thought about this later when I was lying in bed and I asked Sammi the next day whether he knew what tribe he was from. He said "of course" – and shrugged his shoulders.

"Well I don't." I said.

"All I know is that I am from a circus family and

my mother's and father's families were all circus people, from as far back as we could remember."

"That's because you are gypsies." Sammi said and I didn't like the way he said the word 'gypsy.' I had only ever heard the word since I arrived at this camp and it was never spoken in a pleasant way; the word was almost spat out, as if it disgusted the orator.

Sammi noticed my face sadden and gave his annoying laugh. He playfully put his arm around my shoulder and said,

"It just means traveller, that's all. Your family had no fixed abode; really the authorities were doing you a favour by bringing you here, you would all have surely perished if not."

How incredibly mad that statement made me! I took off through the fence like the wind, I was so furious. I arrived at Eden, sat on the grass and caught my breath. How dare he, how dare he? How dare Sammi say those things? My family has been split up; I will never see Mama again and do not want to think what happened to her or our dear animals that were like family to us. And now to find out dear Papa has died too; it was all too much and I sobbed my heart out and dried my tears on the grass.

After lunch I decided to talk to Ummi about it; I wouldn't mention to her what Sammi had said about the Konubo tribe, just about what he said about the authorities doing me a favour by bringing me here. I asked Ummi – how can that be kind when I have lost all freedom and do not know what has happened to my brother?

"I don't know child," she answered, gently stroking my hair. I moved closer to her.

"Our country is at war, there are many complications; do you know what a traitor is?"

I shook my head.

"A traitor is someone who betrays your trust. Remember that my child, you are here on your own and not everyone is trustworthy; there are a lot of wicked people here, many wicked people."

Ummi looked up at the sky with a glazed over expression on her face. I left her to her thoughts for a while although I was very curious as to what she meant and to whom she was referring to as wicked. Ummi's sister Muti eventually broke the silence and inquired about Dopo.

"My daughter Mahiana sometimes manages to deliver a letter to her husband who is living in the men's quarters; she has got to know one of the cooks and she manages to smuggle the letter in. She obviously has to be careful but if you write to Dopo I will ask her to see what she can do next time she writes a letter to her husband. Then maybe you can have some answers and that might just help you to regain some peace in that troubled mind of yours. Happiness comes from within; you are still a child, whatever is happening with your body. You have so much left to learn, I am always here for you and I will try and help you as much as I possibly can. This is a terrible situation, we have to all stick together and try and make the best of life. I wake up each morning and thank God He has brought me safely through the night. Then

I thank Him for the day ahead and pray that I may be useful to Him in whatever way He sees fit to use me. It helps; it takes your thoughts away from yourself. Here, I will fetch you some paper and a pen and you can write to Dopo, let him know you are safe and well, he must be worried about you too."

It took me several days to finish my letter to Dopo, even though in the end it was only a short letter and very precise. I realised how much I had taken his presence for granted, how we just assumed we would not be parted so did not have to discuss our connection. Had we really discussed anything at all? I was beginning to wonder. You don't have to say to someone 'I love you' when by the fact that you are all part of the same family and living together in harmony, being there for each other and showing kindness is love in itself and every day demonstrated that love. Now I was struggling to put words onto paper – why? Because this awful place had invaded my mind, like worms that eat food when it has been left in the sun for too long. That made me angry too; I used to love writing – in my previous life.

When I shut my eyes I could picture Dopo's face – his wide, innocent eyes. We could communicate simply by looking at each other, just the way he tilted his head or the way one side of his mouth would go up slightly – those simple expressions portrayed so much and spoke so many words without speaking any. I felt so close to Dopo that it made my skin tingle and yet I didn't feel the same about Papa and I didn't know why. I had always thought that when someone dies you sense that person around you and maybe dream about them or feel them prompting you to do a certain thing or go a certain way; but I even found it hard to picture Papa's face.

    I was glad when I finally finished my letter and handed it to Muti. I had found the whole experience exhausting and allowed myself a couple of afternoon naps to recover from it. Then I put the letter out of my mind. I did not want to raise my hopes of seeing Dopo again; I wasn't even sure that my letter would reach him.

CHAPTER 9

A week later at dinner Mahiana whispered to me –

"It's been delivered."

Fortunately I had just finished eating as immediately as she spoke the words I felt butterflies skipping around inside my tummy and as hard as I tried I could not think about anything else for days. I imagined Dopo first receiving the letter, holding it in his trembling hands, savouring the moment of opening it, him imagining me writing it, and then reading it over and over again with tears running down his face.

I knew so very little about the day to day lives in the men's side of this camp; we were very much separated. I often heard about the men being driven early each morning to work down the mines but whether that was true or not I had no evidence. There were thousands of people here and new arrivals appeared each day. Personally I was glad I had the Rufaro family living opposite me, at least I felt some degree of stability. I could not fathom or get my head around the fact that the reason I was being snubbed when I went to the canteen or laundry room was because

I associated with my dear neighbours who had shown me nothing but kindness. My thirteen year old brain just could not figure that one out.

The days dragged on with their usual monotony and I tried to blot out thoughts of hearing from Dopo and the only time I allowed myself to think about him was when I laid in bed at the end of the day. Then I would dream about what it would be like to meet up with him again. It had been over a year now that we had been at Dahagey; I invented an imaginary picture in my head of Dopo with a beard and moustache, looking all grown up. The picture brought a smile to my face and the day dream meant that I went to sleep happy and it had been a long time since I could say that.

Dopo and I had always got along but I think because we were never apart for more than a few hours we just accepted that we would always be there for one another and when something or someone is that familiar you don't necessarily consider life without them and the same applied to Mama and Papa. Although Dopo was younger than me he was stocky and strong and would have no problem working long, gruelling days down the mine; if indeed this was the case. I had no fear about that or that he would grow weak from our meagre food rations; he was young and always maintained a cheerful disposition and I felt sure that he would take everything that was thrust upon him with all the exuberance that only youth could provide. Having said that, if he knew about Papa and I cannot see why he wouldn't as I had found out – how would that affect him? Had he been relying on Papa this last year and not been as independent as I had been? How I longed to be able to comfort him, to help and support him at this harrowing time of his life. We were orphans as I have no doubt that dear Mama would have suffered the same fate as our dear animals.

I did not want to pester the Rufaro family with constant questions about news of Dopo; I knew they would inform me if they had heard anything, they knew how desperate I was and how lonely I felt. I would have appreciated understanding how the system of letter giving worked. Who did Mahiana give the letter to? Then what happened? Did they just ask around whether anyone knew Dopo Okeke?

A few days later the opportunity arose. Mahiana and I were doing our laundry and she was telling a funny story about her younger brother. Apparently he was walking along talking to his friend when he bumped into a post that had just been erected. Mahiana said the funny thing was as he looked around dazed he said – "who put that post there?" Personally I didn't see the humour of the situation but I saw an opening to ask about Dopo. So staying on the subject of brothers I enquired –

"Is there any news on Dopo, anything at all?"

Mahiana paused her vigorous rubbing of her clothes and turned to face me.

"No, my child; I am truly sorry. I asked my source the other day and he said he has looked everywhere and checked every list and there is nothing, no mention of him at all. I'm sorry, I have done all I can do."

"That's crazy," I shouted, "that doesn't make sense.

Dopo arrived with me, there must be some record."

Mahiana dried her hands on her apron and came over to me and put her arm round my shoulder.

"I know you are frustrated Marna and I understand. Most people here, including myself have lost loved ones; I know how hard it is for you when you have nobody around you who is dear to you. There are so many people here coming and going and there are endless lists. Just the other day a man was looking for his young son but he could not read or write and nobody could interpret his dialect so it was impossible to spell the boy's name. The father went all around the camp calling for his son until he had no voice left.

This is how it is here – we have no voice. This is a camp of suffering. Nobody knows our names save our loved ones. If you don't mind me saying Marna, there are many people here who have suffered far greater than you. That is why most people keep their heads down and only speak if necessary. Many children here are selective mutes and live in a silent world inside themselves where they hope that if they don't speak either the memories will go away or that it was all just a horrible dream. Whatever they have suffered has shocked them into silence, it happens a lot."

I looked up at Mahiana and as I looked into her kind face I felt my eyes welling up and big teardrops fell onto my chest – tears of frustration and loneliness. I smiled at her as I know she meant well and was only trying to help.

"Try your hardest to be positive my child, think of all the things you can be grateful for, even if it is just a tiny thing. Who knows maybe one day you will be Marna the Magnificent again, flying through the air with a packed arena all clapping and cheering your name. Keep practising your cartwheels and splits, keep yourself supple and keep believing. You are young, you won't be here forever, you have so much life ahead of you and I think that you can be a great help to others here if you were to put your mind to it."

I was beyond consoling. I didn't want to think about helping others, I wanted to be like the mute children, they clammed up because it was all too much. I didn't care what Mahiana's 'source' said, Dopo had to be somewhere, I can't just be alone in this world. I skipped dinner and lay looking at the slight hole in the middle of my tent where the pole sat. It didn't matter what time of day or season it was there were always some insects hovering around that hole. It was like they knew that was the way of escape, the way out to the open air but couldn't quite work out the next step in the path to freedom.

Then as I lay motionless a strange thing happened; I gradually stopped feeling sorry for myself and I thought about what Mahiana had said. In all these weeks that I had been so fixated on finding out about Dopo's whereabouts and thinking about him I had become blinkered. I had stopped noticing my surroundings; I hadn't really said thank you properly to Sammi for giving me the jumper and blanket. Yes this was a place of suffering with suffering people inside but we were people nevertheless.

We were a community of sorts and I knew from being here over a year that the worst thing to do was to crawl up inside of yourself; we had to stick together and try and help each other. I don't know how long Sammi had been working here but in his small, quiet way he was trying his best to look out for people; even if it meant he could get into trouble.

By the time I had finished my musings it was starting to get dark. I got up and took a slow walk to the latrines. I resolved to tell Sammi how grateful I was to him and I would thank Mahiana too. Her positive thinking had kicked in already!

CHAPTER 10

Sammi predictably laughed when I tried to thank him.

"You know your problem my pretty one? You spend too much time in that head of yours; you should be jumping and stretching and whatever else you gymnasts do. I heard that you missed dinner last night, that won't do, that won't do at all. I don't want you getting skinny and wasting away. I don't want to feel your ribs under your pretty jumper do I?

As he spoke the last remark he touched my ribs.

"Ouch!"

"See what I mean?" laughed Sammi, ever the joker.

" I want to see you eat all your dinner up tonight."

So with my new Samaritan outlook I continued on my days. I found some attractive little stones at Eden and invented a simple game. I drew five circles in the dirt with my finger making the shape of a flower and the idea was that you threw a stone into each of the 'petals' and then you threw a stone to land in the middle circle.

Mary Daniels

I thought it was a very simple game that any age group could understand and it could be adapted if you drew a different shape in the dirt. I put the stones in my pocket and brought them back to Dahagey. After lunch I sat on a patch of dirt and started to draw my flower and throw the stones. It did not take long for some curious children to have a look at what I was doing – I smiled at them and asked if they wanted to play. It really did not matter whether they spoke or not and we spent hours, sometimes the whole afternoon playing my simple game. I had to find another colourful stone as one little girl refused to let go of hers. She just sat still and silently turned the shiny stone over slowly in her hands. Another little girl would come up to me and position herself determinedly onto my lap. It was like she was saying – you have no choice, I am sitting on your lap and I am staying here. I need to feel a body close to me. And that was fine; I quite enjoyed the sensation too.

I was scared to form any close relationships with these dear children, scared that I would love them so much that they became a part of me and if we were separated a part of me would be separated too and I wasn't sure I had the strength to deal with that raw hurt. But they were very sweet! I think they really appreciated the distraction to the boredom of their days and also a distraction to their traumatic memories and situation they found themselves in. So if I was contributing in any small way in helping these fragile, little lives and helping them endure their stay here at Dahagey then that made me happy.

All this meant that gradually I stopped thinking about Dopo, he was still in my heart of course and I still felt the strange sensation that he was constantly nearby. I could see his smile as I played with the children and that was a pleasant feeling. I thought about these things as I went to bed and it almost made me content.

One afternoon as I was walking back to my tent having been with the children a while a young man called out my name from across the fence.

"Hey Marna," he called.

"Is your surname Okeke?"

"It is, yes, it is a very common name as you know."

"I know it is but Marna is not a common name and there is a man in the men's section who is asking about you. Don't ask me any more details because that is all I know. If you like I can arrange a meeting but I don't have any other details so don't go raising your hopes."

And with that he ran off.

CHAPTER 11

The next few weeks were a bit of a blur; there were so many confusing things happening all at once that the only place where I felt at peace was when I went to Eden. How I ached to linger there longer than was able, I could easily and happily live there and I dreamt about it as I lay flat on the green grass by the clear, pure well. I thought to myself I have clean water here and I can shelter under the trees and there is nobody here to confuse me or lie to me; how beautiful and uncomplicated life would be if I never had to leave here. This was my dream but my reality was so very different.

The man who had approached me and knew my name apparently had some connection with Kali and she gingerly spoke to me one day at dinner and said that she was looking into it for me. Kali managed to gather together some information and a meeting was arranged for me to meet with whoever it was who was asking after me. The meeting was arranged for the following Sunday morning – early – as the green shirts often partied on Saturday nights and were not quite as vigilant and alert on a Sunday morning as they might have been on other mornings. Kali showed me where the man – who I hoped with every ounce of my being was Dopo – would be waiting. It was in an area that was in the farthest western corner of the camp where the ground had been too sandy and loose to put the stakes in for the fence. There was a piece of ground about ten feet square there. It had a few gorse bushes on it and there was a gap between the fence posts from the men's half and the women and children's half and this was where the meeting was to be held.

Just thinking about Sunday morning sent a million butterflies fluttering around in my tummy; it had been such a long time since I had seen any members of my family. I was too nervous for words and in the days leading up to Sunday I flitted about from one activity to the next like an excited mosquito. I shared my news with the Rufaros and told them that hopefully there was to be a happy ending after all and I would meet Dopo. Then one day after lunch, as I ran up to our tents, their tent was shut up and the woven mats that stayed outside permanently had disappeared and the whole area was deserted. I literally froze on the spot – what had happened? They were here this morning and they didn't say anything, just the usual wave and greeting. I had only been away for a few hours, this was so strange. So many emotions were swirling around in my head and I had no one to confide in. this place was so incredibly infuriating. I crawled into my tent and curled up into a ball on my bed with my head faced down on the pillow. I went to supper but nobody said anything about where the Rufaros had gone. I was totally flummoxed.

I managed to sleep for a few hours that night out of

pure mental exhaustion and in the stillness that is found only in the small hours of the morning I tried to process the events of the previous day. Why would the Rufaros move and why, if they were being moved did they not inform me? We had become close over the last few months, I was especially close to Ummi. I loved waking up in the morning to the sound of the children playing and laughing – the way only children can. To live in a canvas shack with barely adequate food and water – and nothing else – and to laugh and play the way they did gave me a reason to get up in the morning, especially since I had invented my little stone game. I would untie the rope that kept my door shut and blink as the strong sunlight hit my eyes only to be greeted with their warm smiles and dirty hands. Now, as I lay in bed I knew that as the sun started to wake up I would hear nothing. Ummi had made their tent really homely and decorated it with colourful material on the walls and cushions on the floor. Also it was one of the largest tents in this camp, if not the biggest so what would make them suddenly up and leave? No matter how much I tried to analyse the situation I came to the conclusion that nothing made sense and all I hoped was that I would be enlightened as to what happened and hopefully see my friendly neighbours again.

"Hey Sammi." I called out nonchalantly the following morning.

"Well hello my little ray of sunshine. Why do you only have one container today?"

"Oh dear, I was hoping you could answer that for me Sammi. I have no idea what has happened but the Rufaros have disappeared, they are not in their tent and they weren't at breakfast. Have you heard anything?"

Sammi shook his head.

"I don't know," he said but as I walked through my familiar gap in the fence and made my way to my beloved Eden something told me he was lying and that he knew an awful lot more than he was letting on.

I mechanically drudged through the day with the thought of never seeing Ummi or the dear little children again depressing me more and more each time the thought entered my mind. And as I dawdled slowly back to my tent at the end of day I was met by my new neighbours; an elderly couple who both looked so frail I doubted they would last the winter. They looked like skeletons dressed in rags. I half smiled at them as I passed but I was determined not to befriend them as not only could I not bear to lose anybody else but also I really did not have the energy to strike up conversation.

By the time Sunday arrived I had such a range of emotions inside of me with each one rearing its head like the children's toy that has a weatherman who pops up with a windy face, then that goes down and a sunny face appears or a rainy face, that was how I felt. Yes, just the slightest chance of seeing my brother again filled me with such a joy; just the thought of finally having somebody to connect with and know he was alright was totally overwhelming. And yet there were also emotions of sadness and anger mixed with my old friends hopelessness and despair. I had spent over a year trying not to meditate on the future and yet now I felt there was a glimmer of hope and just maybe there would be a life for me and my brother beyond Dahagey.

It was as I was in this state that I made my way at pre-dawn to the no-man's area at the western corner of the camp. I stood nervously waiting for what felt like ages, the air was chilly and I looked around continually hoping to see some movement of life until eventually I did see a figure approaching. He was hurrying along and before I knew it he came right up to my face. This definitely wasn't how I imagined things would be because it wasn't Dopo who approached me but Papa! Now my head was really spinning and I was suddenly wide awake. Papa was alive – I was so elated – but he was not elated – he was angry – very angry – very angry indeed.

"Papa, Papa, I thought you were dead."

I managed to stammer amidst tears of elation but also shock. I tried to hug him but he pushed me away – hard.

"You are not a daughter to me, you are a disgrace."

Papa yelled in my face. Now my tears were streaming down my face. This was supposed to be the happiest event that had happened to me since arriving in this forlorn place. Now Papa would not even hug me. He continued his rant, standing so near to my face I could see the white of his eyes and smell his breath.

"How could you associate with that despicable Rufaro family? They are our enemy, you stupid, ignorant girl. Don't you understand? You should not have so much as spoken to them. They killed Dopo. Dopo is dead and I want nothing more to do with you, do you understand?

Nothing, no more letters, I am disgusted by you, I can't even look at you."

And with that he walked off, out of my life forever.

CHAPTER 12

The elderly couple, as I foresaw, did not survive very long and in their place came a noisy, screaming family consisting of two sisters who constantly argued and five – I think – small children who were mainly left to their own devices. I laid in my tent and wished they would all be quiet, even if just for a day. I was adamant that I was not going to get to know them and avoided them at all costs, even to the point of waiting until they went inside their tent or walked away before I ventured out of mine. And so it was that my miserable life continued. I stopped going every day to collect water, it was only for me and I stopped myself thinking about my new noisy neighbours whenever I went to Eden. I thought to myself – I am just caring about myself now. I had seen so many people go downhill very rapidly here and I did not want to be another statistic. I had no one left, everyone that I had loved and given my love to had either died, betrayed me or lied to me and I had had enough.

Something died in me the day I saw my father (he didn't deserve to be called Papa anymore.) There was a part of me, deep down in my very soul that became numb that early morning when I went to no-man's land and as

I walked away and witnessed the most glorious sunrise I very much doubted that that part of me would ever be revisited or resurrected. And as I woke up on subsequent mornings I thought – why? Why bother? Why bother to collect water for somebody else or look out for anyone? This thinking was all very well but without starting the day by thinking about someone you care for or doing a deed for someone other than yourself made life quite worthless. Obviously I thought long and hard about what my father had accused the Rufaros of but I could never picture the scene; I preferred to think of Dopo sleeping peacefully in somewhere beautiful like Eden, eternally at rest without having to deal with this terrible, torturous life. And even if it was a member of the Rufaro family that had committed the terrible crime of murder, it didn't mean that the family I became friends with were involved in any way. It could just have been a black sheep in the family as the saying goes. I think all families have these and it doesn't make the whole family guilty. I certainly did not want to associate myself with my father anymore after that meeting and the way he got in my face and was so nasty and callous towards me. I did not want to be affiliated with him in any way and if anyone asked about my family from now on I would shake my head and say – no I do not have a father or any family member alive.

One question it did answer was why I felt Dopo's presence with me but not my dead-to-me father and in a strange way I found it comforting to think of Dopo sitting in heaven watching over me. I found myself asking him when in a certain situation – what would you do Dopo?

The weather was starting to heat up and the sun's power was becoming intense. The heavy canvas of which our tents were made was not designed for these conditions and you would wake up sweltering even before the sun's strength had peaked. It was quite unbearable; in the winter the nights were chilly and there was no insulation at all in these makeshift spaces and however much love and care a person – normally a woman – put into making a home – a home they were not. I was so fed up, there was never any space you could call your own and Dahagey grew more and more crowded and it was impossible to have any privacy. The only place I managed to find any form of solace was either in my tent or at Eden. First of all I started missing the odd day to collect water then two days went by and I made my water last. One day when I had not been to Eden and missed lunch, I was lying in my baking hot tent with the door open when who should peer round the corner? Sammi, I wasn't sure if I was pleased to see him or not, we had hardly spoken since 'the incident.' I think he rightly perceived that I really did not want to talk about it and so apart from a one syllable greeting each morning we had hardly communicated. I tried to question him about why he told me father had died but he said he genuinely had been informed that on good authority and looked quite hurt at the notion that I could have believed he would lie to me.

"Hey you." He smiled as his poked his head through the opening of the door.

"Hey sleepy head, I brought you a sandwich."

He came in and I shifted my legs to swing over the

side of the camp bed and he sat down on the end of the bed.

"I have been worried about you," he began. I was really not in the mood for any of this and I sighed whilst nonchalantly picking up my sandwich.

"Eat up, it was either that or a woolly jumper, would you have preferred that?"

"I am really not in the mood Sammi. I am here and I am fine, as you can see; you really do not need to fuss over me."

"Charming – is that all the thanks I get for putting myself out for you? Have you any idea the trouble I could get in? Even by coming here to your tent could get me the sack – but no – little Miss madam just lies in her own filth wallowing in self-pity. She can't even pretend to laugh at my jokes."

He nudged my arm but I was in no mood to go along with him. The last thing I wanted was to argue or feel bad about myself. I just wanted him to leave, it felt like he was invading my space and I didn't like it. I didn't like it one little bit.

"I am sorry Sammi, you have been a good friend to me; I need to get out of this place, there are so many people here now, I feel as if my head is about to explode. Is there no one who can help me get out of here? I cannot bear to stay here for another stifling summer."

"I just don't want to see you go under; we have known each other for some time now. The first time I saw you I knew that you were different – and it wasn't just because you did great cartwheels! I recognised a fighting spirit in you and I thought – that girl will go far, she's got guts. But you were alone and vulnerable and there are many bad people here. I don't think you are aware of a lot of what goes on here and I'm glad you don't, but I have tried to look out for you and protect you, no matter what danger that puts me in. You know what your name means don't you?"

I nodded and he moved a bit closer.

"Never give up, never give up Marna."

That was the first time ever that he had called me by my name, emotions welled up inside of me that I desperately tried to keep under control. Sammi stood up and leaning over me almost whispered –

"I will be your Papa – if you like – would you like that, then you wouldn't need to feel so alone?"

I shrugged and nodded meekly. He walked away with a big grin on his face.

CHAPTER 13

In time I recovered from my wallowing and tried to find at least one thing a day to make me smile, even if it was just a tiny thing; I would go to bed at night and set my mind to think on one lovely thing that had happened or that I had seen. Often it was a flower that had bloomed overnight at Eden or the way the sunbeams sparkled on the water there. Other times it was a child's smile or their funny antics but most of the time it was something I had seen at Eden. I had begun to do an exercise routine when I went to Eden and although it was very hot it somehow invigorated me to stretch and remember the workouts that I did at the circus – which seemed a million years ago now. I would rush back with my water, just about making it in time for lunch. One day Sammi said to me –

"I don't know what you do at that place where you get water, you take ages and you are always so hot and sweaty – not very ladylike at all!"

He laughed and ruffled my matted hair before continuing in a more serious note.

"You aren't a little girl anymore you know, your body is changing, you are growing up and could be an attractive young lady with just a little effort."

"Whatever you say Sammi, it's just hot, that's all."

"Yes I know, the sun is very strong especially in the middle of the day; but I'm alright, I am going home to enjoy an ice cold coca-cola from my fridge and sit in my cool air-conditioned house."

My eyes were as wide as saucers.

"Really Sammi? I can't imagine anything more wonderful, that must be so refreshing; everything here is warm – warm and tasteless. I haven't had anything chilled since I came here."

"Oh my dear, sweet princess! I'd love to take you out of this place; my Ummi would spoil you rotten!"

"I've resigned myself to this camp, I am just trying to exist as best as I can, taking one day at a time and living in hope that one day, somehow, a way of escape will open up for me; but for now that is all I can do and if I allow myself to start thinking about cold drinks and air con it will drive me mad – literally."

"Yeah well I'm sorry okay. I am not responsible for this soulless place, these endless rows of sweltering tents and the war that put you here in the first place."

I sighed deeply and replied.

"I have to go, I do not want to indulge in thoughts about changing my circumstances or what might have been if maybe we had moved on before we were captured and brought here. Those thoughts are not healthy."

"Alright my brave little lady, go and fetch your lunch, I might have a surprise for you tomorrow."

He winked at me and I ran off. It was Sunday and the queue outside Dahagey was longer than ever. What would happen to all these people I wondered? Would the separated men, the good and honest fathers who had worked hard all their lives to support their wives and children, ever get to see them again? Would they ever regain some form of normal family life? And how was anybody going to take notice of me? I am just one small cog in a very large wheel, one that is out of control with no resources or ideas of how to fix it. Somehow the conversation with Sammi left me with the desolate emotions I was constantly fighting against to hold back. Why should his life be so different? Did it make any sense for me to continue hoping in this hopeless place?

As much as I tried to think about anything other than the glass of coca-cola with ice cubes in and the coolness of the air conditioning I still found myself dwelling upon these things as I settled down for the night. I couldn't include that in my 'nice thing of the day' list because it hadn't happened to me and was pretty unlikely to. Then my old friend depression rose up because I couldn't think of anything nice at all that had happened that day. I had twisted my ankle at Eden and it was still sore and when I shut my eyes all I saw was the endless line of dull-eyed, stooped over, hungry, desperate, displaced people. I slept fitfully that night.

As I stepped down on the hard ground the next morning my ankle throbbed; it was too hot to stay in my tent so I hobbled to a partially shady spot and lay down on my mat. I felt as if all my energy had sapped away, 'maybe I should lie in the sun and shrivel away – like a big sultana'

I thought. But I didn't and after a couple of hours I felt better. I was walking across the camp to do my laundry when I heard a familiar voice calling to me.

"I looked out for you, I told you I had a surprise for you but it's ruined now."

I wanted to run – anywhere – away from Sammi's negativity and uncanny knack of making me feel bad, but running was not an option with my sore ankle.

"I brought you a slice of chocolate cake, we had it last night after our Sunday dinner but it is melted now."

I shrugged and disappeared around the laundry block; I stopped when I knew he was out of sight and realised I hadn't spoken to him – or anyone else actually all day. However hard I thrashed about washing my clothes I could not get the image of a slice of chocolate cake out of my mind and as I was alone in my tent that night I salivated at the thought of oozing, sweet chocolate melting on my tongue. I wished I did not know how delicious this feeling was then I wouldn't be experiencing such disappointment. Why did Sammi have to tell me? It wasn't as if I didn't feel bad enough already. I must have fallen to sleep trying to remember the last time I had tasted anything flavoursome because I woke up with the same thought in my head but reprimanded myself saying – be grateful Marna, you are safe and at least you have food, there are many, many people far worse off than you. Now get up, it is a new day.

And a very good new day it turned out to be as well as when I met Sammi he had a huge grin going from one side of his face to the other. He held out his hands in which he held a paper bag. I took the bag gingerly and peeked inside but before I saw what it was the sweet aroma hit my salivary glands – a square of raisin cake – how divine. I saved it until I reached Eden and lay on my tummy on the green, luscious grass and took my time enjoying every single crumb. This must be what people feel after they partake of a long fast I thought to myself, the flavours seemed so pronounced and incredibly sweet. It had been the longest time since I had tasted anything so delicious.

After that day Sammi had a paper bag for me each morning; I would give him the empty one when I came through the fence with my water and the next day he had something sweet for me. Yes this was a kind gesture of his, it was thoughtful and I was always aware of not being ungrateful; yet I always felt that whenever Sammi gave me anything it came with a price. I couldn't quite explain the way I felt and knew that if I mentioned it to anyone they would say – oh how can you even think such a thing? Sammi is a good man, he is just looking out for you and trying to improve your stay here in whatever small way he is able to. They were right but there were mornings when I wished that he wouldn't bring me his paper bag – or actually that he was not there at all. Were there other girls that he treated this way? Was I the only one? I did ask him once but he did his usual predictable routine of turning my enquiry into a joke and laughingly said I was his one and only special girl, didn't I know that?

CHAPTER 14

I had started to spot some members of the Rufaro family when I went to the canteen – not the same ones who lived opposite me, that will forever remain a mystery where they ended up but I knew these people were relatives who belonged to the family. They would sit on a big table and always look so happy and they always looked out for each other. How could they have killed Dopo? What could have happened to make them so mad? Sammi said that they were a notorious, violent family and my father had said the same thing. I wanted to run over to them and thump my fist on their table and scream – what happened? Tell me, tell me now; what did my sweet, innocent brother ever do to you to make you have so much hatred in your heart that it incited you to murder him? Father said it was a family feud but that just did not make sense. The Rufaro family were lovely; I lived opposite to them for over a year and saw nothing but kindness and care. They braided my hair and I missed that act of affection and our conversations. The other thing was that if they were a family of love and our families were at war with each other then what did that make our family? The one that raised me and taught me the principles of life; the one that I thought was trustworthy and true.

I tried to make sure that I sat away from them when I went to the canteen; I found the whole thing so confusing and absolutely maddening and it made me hate Dahagey with a passionate loathing that rose up from my stomach and made it difficult for me to digest my food – which wasn't an easy task at the best of times! If I could I choose a seat in a corner of the huge, canvas canteen and avoided personal contact with anybody as much as possible and always kept my head down to avoid eye contact. I fooled myself into believing that this state of affairs was the best way of going about my days and I reasoned that if nobody came into my personal space and I was left alone then nobody would upset me or let me down.

This was true and was all well and good but in behaving thus and shutting everyone out I became morbid and isolated. Sammi noticed it and repeatedly commented how worried he was about me but as the summer wore on – and wore on it did; especially as in the unbearable heat it was impossible to stay inside your tent as soon as it was daylight – it was torture and yet being outside all day with no privacy was also torture. My only solace was Eden – and how I loved it there. I would lie on the grass and let my thoughts wander; sometimes they would wander into the future – but that was a blank canvas. I remember as a child going with my father to a printing shop to print out posters and flyers for the circus and if something went wrong with the printer then the page would come out blank with nothing printed onto it – and this is what I saw when I allowed my thoughts to meander into a time frame that was beyond Dahagey. How could I contemplate anything beyond this cage, this life?

Oh if only I could live at Eden, how wonderful and simply perfect life would be!

A day arrived, a day I will never forget when all my illusions were shattered. It began the same way that any day began and I walked up to Eden, my favourite place, my haven where I felt I could take a deep breath and breathe freely again. I felt like the air was free and as I looked up towards the cloudless, blue sky I inhaled slowly, enjoying this wonderful, silent tranquillity. My body drooped in appreciation and I lay down on the luscious grass; marvelling at the bright, succulent shoots bursting with life and optimism. I was so grateful to be able to come to this private solace and that made what happened that morning even more distressing and painful; because what happened was that Sammi had secretly followed me – yes, he followed me to my beloved Eden. My secret place had now been violated, he had tainted it forever. I sat up and screamed in shock.

"Hey, calm down, I was curious alright, I'm allowed to be curious you know! "

Then he grinned his stupid, white-teethed smile.

"Why are you here Sammi? " I asked softly, trying to control my breathing so as not to have a panic attack.

"I'm worried about you, you know I am. I've been watching out for you for a long time now. I am worried you are going to slip under. This seems to be the only time you show any enthusiasm when you come here. So I was curious as to what you did up here, I know it doesn't take that long to draw water from the well – and here you are lying about on the grass. So is that it, is this your big mystery? "

I was shaking as my seething anger longed to rise up and scream and push Sammi away – away from My Eden but the damage had been done already and I was cross. I was cross with Sammi's audacity to follow me here, cross with my hopeless situation and cross that I had slipped up enough for Sammi to be able to intrude into my privacy, my only remaining place of sanity. Sammi sat down on the grass and moved towards me so that he was close enough to be able to whisper to me and I could hear.

"Listen, I am worried about your welfare, I must care about you, mustn't I? I have walked all the way out here I this scorching heat, I wouldn't do that unless I cared, would I? It's just not healthy, this - what you are doing." He waved his hand vaguely over the area of Eden and carried on.

"This isn't a life my sweet, this is escapism. You have lost your spark. I know how difficult things have been for you lately, which is why I have tried to cheer you up with my cakes. And I know how Dahagey gets to you, especially when you have been here for a while – everything becomes monotonous and you operate on automatic pilot but if you don't get yourself out of that rut and pull yourself together you very soon fall apart. I have been here long enough, I have seen it happen. First you see the light go out of a person's eye, then they quickly descend into 'zombie-ism' if that's a word, do you think that's a word my little dreamer, what do you think?"

He nudged me in a friendly way and I half smiled. I had calmed down by this point. He was trying and what he said made me think. He continued.

"And you know what happens after zombie-ism, don't you? You have witnessed it for yourself far too many times; you have seen things nobody should see, especially not at your tender age. I know you have lost a lot of friends – good people who just give up on living and that is the point I don't want to see you get to."

He took hold of my hand and helped me up. It did make sense what he had spoken; I had lost a lot of loved ones but what was the answer? We walked back to Dahagey in silence and it reminded me of when we used to move our circus on. We all had our jobs to do and gradually everything was dismantled until the marquee became a crumpled mass on the ground – and that is what I felt like – a flattened, crumpled mass. The only time of the day I looked forward to coming to Eden and now that was ruined. If Sammi could follow me once he could do it again; I would never be able to relax.

My daydreaming about circus days was suddenly interrupted as I was aware of Sammi speaking to me.

"Ummi was asking about you, you know. She asked me who I was giving the extra cakes to and I told her about you. She said she would love to meet you, she said it was sad that you have been here on your own for such a long time and with no family. I always think about you when we sit with our cold drinks in the air conditioned room."

The next sentence Sammi spoke slowly, looking me in the eye.

" I have been thinking about it, how to get you out of here. We would have to do it at night, sneak you out somehow, what do you think? You deserve better than this, if it wasn't for me nobody else would look after you, especially now you've gone into your shell, you realise that don't you?"

I answered with mono-syllables and waited until I was in my bed before I digested this awful day. The question that seemed to pop out at me was 'why did Sammi say he had to sneak me out?' There were people I knew who had legitimately left here with their papers. They either found jobs or a family member came to take them to safety so why couldn't Sammi get me out properly? Why did we have to weasel out in the dead of night? I couldn't understand it and I didn't want to leave here like that, not in that way. I had often dreamed about walking out of here, through the large, impending gates with my head held high but of course that was when I thought I had a family still. So why couldn't Sammi get me out of here legally? I went to sleep with this thought and woke up with it being my first thought of the day. As I lay still in the early pre-dawn light, before the world awakes I pondered all that Sammi had spoken about the day and I came to the conclusion that if that was the way that Sammi said it had to be and if this was my chance of escape, of a new life, then I should grab onto it with everything I have. When I used to ask Sammi lots of questions he would often say – "you overthink things too much" – and maybe he is right. He certainly had my best interests at heart and has gone out of his way on numerous occasions when he really did not have to and there was nothing in it for him. So I must trust that for whatever reason we had to escape at night. The very thought of it sent butterflies fluttering in my tummy.

And so I sprung out of bed with a skip in my step which I thought I had lost forever. I ate my meals heartedly and daydreamed constantly of leaving here. I kept saying to myself – this could be the last time I have breakfast here or the last time I do my laundry or go to collect water at Eden and even that didn't bother me now as I could begin to truly dream of my future. Sammi laughed when he saw me.

"Wow what has happened to you my flower? Have you began to blossom?"

Normally I would cringe at such a sleazy comment and hurry on through the broken fence as fast as I could but today I smiled broadly and very briefly hugged him. I knew this was not at all appropriate behaviour towards green shirts. They were there to keep things in order and they kept their distance from the refugees but I wanted to show Sammi how much I appreciated him and what he was trying to do for me.

Over the next two weeks Sammi and I worked out our escape. I only saw him for a few minutes a day and often he was with another green shirt so we had to be brief. He told me a little about his family. His father had passed away ten years ago and his brother was working in the city and sent home what he could to help the family. There were three sisters at home also so Sammi said that his Ummi said having another girl at home was no problem. He showed me a photograph of his home and it brought tears to my eyes, not because it was in any way beautiful or special but just because it was a home and I had not seen or been inside a home or part of a family for a year and a half. I told Sammi to tell his Ummi that I would do everything she told me to do and whatever jobs needed doing I would do them and help as best I could.

Oh how naïve was I and how little I knew that my words would come back to haunt me.

Part Two
The Absorption

Mary Daniels

of the Burden

CHAPTER 15

So this is my story, I am sixteen years old now and apparently worth less money than I was when I was younger and my body was just starting to develop. When I left Dahagey I was pretty much uneducated but Adeleine and Benito taught me how to read and write properly and now I just love reading! I cannot imagine life without reading books – but then I could not imagine having any life at all at one time, when I was at my lowest.

I used to make myself do one hundred press ups a day, even if I was completely exhausted, and I was often. I was determined to stay strong and if I had to run a hundred miles to escape, I wanted to be as fit as possible and not get out of breath and recaptured. The only good thing about my three years of hell was that the food was reasonable, as Sammi always said he didn't want skinny girls; no man wanted to see a girl's bones he would say.

I never went to Sammi's house. We escaped Dahagey and jumped into his jeep. He told me to get in the back and keep my head down. Periodically he would glance back and smile.

"It is not much further my princess, have a sleep if you like, Ummi is dying to meet you."

We did not stop, he gave me a small bottle of water but soon my mouth became so dry it was painful to swallow. I had been unable to sleep at all the previous night and, although my whole body was screaming out for sleep, I was becoming increasingly anxious about the situation. Sammi had started to whistle a monotonous tune and it grated on my nerves like a chalk going up and down a blackboard. The same thought circled round and round in my head – Sammi had told me on numerous occasions that he lived five minutes away from Dahagey. This did not add up. By now the sun had risen in the sky and the heat, even with the breeze coming through the window, was unbearable. It was impossible for me to speak to Sammi or get his attention as he was too far away. With every passing minute I was aware that something was VERY wrong. Sammi was behaving like a cat that had the cream – why was he so happy and where the hell were we going?

CHAPTER 16

My next memory is waking up in the dark; my head was pounding and everything seemed foggy somehow. I never saw Sammi again or met his Ummi or sisters. I had been kidnapped, only I had gone into it voluntarily. I had agreed to leave Dahagey without my papers or anyone knowing where I was – or caring. I was completely isolated - I had a vague memory of signing something when we escaped Dahagey through the same hole in the fence that had been my escape for so long and kept my sanity. How ironic was that? Now I was in a prison, trapped in a far worse situation. I heard voices and, as my eyes became accustomed to the darkness, I realised that I was in a cave-like room in the middle of a corridor where there were about twenty rooms, each with a girl like me in. I strained my eyes to see if there was a girl in the room opposite, I tried to stand up but my legs were like jelly. That's when I noticed the blood, trickling down my bare legs and then it was like a heavy stone had planted itself in the pit of my stomach. The stone stayed there for three years, for the time that I was held in that awful place.

After a few weeks I got used to the routine and the realisation that I had two choices; either I went under or I fought to survive. At first I was in a numb stupor and when the disgusting men did their disgusting acts to me I tried my hardest to blot it out. I would go through whole trapeze routines in my head – over and over. Our food was delivered to our rooms most of the time but occasionally we could go out into a fenced in area which was off to the side of the corridor where our cells were. I remember the first time this happened and I was really shocked to see that our captors were not our male 'visitors' but women. We were being held by women – how could this be? How could I have been so ignorant of life? Why didn't I realise that Sammi was just grooming me all along, did he now have his eyes set on another helpless, innocent victim? Was he helping her through the gap in the fence, making her feel special until she was putty in his hands – literally?

The thought of being held by women captors awoke an inner anger in me. I just could not fathom how my fellow sex could stand by idly, knowing full well the daily and nightly torture and abuse my fellow innocent victims and I were suffering. I still escaped into my daydreams when being violated but, in between these torments I would exercise either on the bed or on the floor of my cell; I devised an exercise routine that lasted about half an hour. I tried to do it twice a day. I figured that if there was any hope of escape the stronger and fitter I became the better. How was I in this same situation of longing to escape after all I suffered at Dahagey? But this was different, this was entirely my fault and this conviction of my predicament being of my own making and stupidity drove me to carry on. It woke up the fighting spirit inside me which I had allowed Sammi to suppress for many months. He had a way of making you feel bad about yourself and making you feel like you wanted to constantly repay him; that you always owed him something so in the end you were always treading on egg shells and trying to please him. Now although I was a prisoner in a dark, damp dungeon I was strong. There was a strength inside me that had not died and that nothing could kill – suppress yes but it was alive and I fully intended to feed that strength.

I reasoned that I was in this situation of my own making and if I did not make it out alive I would have nobody to blame but myself.

I do not think that any of the other girls had been there that long as they all appeared to be in shock and if they did speak to each other it was about everyday things like what we had to eat or that they were worried their periods had stopped. This did happen, obviously this happened, and many horrendous things happened. I heard sounds nobody wants to hear and the fact that you are locked away helpless is another form of torture in itself.

One of the things I hated about being separated from the daylight was that it was hard to know what time of day it was. I do not believe that our food was brought to us at the same time each day but we were fed most days three times a day. The brick in my stomach did a somersault when I recalled Sammi joking about not wanting to see my ribs – "men like a bit of meat on a girl you know" – he joked, grinning his famous, wide grin. Now I was the one to grin at the irony as I remembered that I thought he was genuinely looking out for me and that he truly cared.

I would count three meals and then think that another day had gone by. It seemed to be the unwritten law that you did not speak to the women captors or the people who brought our food. These were often small boys, possibly the children of the women captors or maybe children who had been born there. I do not know but I did witness a girl innocently asking one of the women captors a question about another girl and the woman slapped her so hard across the head that her ear bled and I heard her quietly sobbing for days afterwards. So as much as I desperately wanted to know what the date was so that I could have some sort of order to my existence, I dared not ask. I avoided all eye contact with our female captors. Actually they genuinely scared me - I thought to myself that this must be the lowest point to which a human being can fall; to be fully aware of the suffering of your same sex, of the innocent children being constantly molested – and yet choose to turn a blind eye. How hardened must their souls be, to choose to live such a deplorable life?

Obviously girls did die; either by sickness brought on by neglect, or from violence or suicide. The only thing that kept me from the latter was that I would not let Sammi have the satisfaction of thinking he had won. Once I got into my exercise routine and noticed my muscles building again I began to feel like I could face a new day. It made me feel in control; even if it was just this one area of my survival, it was better than nothing. I think it was to my advantage that I was used to being on my own. I saw a lot of girls go under; I think a lot of that weakness was because they had never spent much time by themselves or had to make decisions for themselves - or cope on their own; whereas I had lived that way for almost a year and a half at Dahagey. So, however lonely I felt, it was not a new sensation to me. I did not make any friends in my time of hell and it wasn't until Adeleine and Benito came into my life that I had any significant conversations at all.

There was one room which I personally never entered but I was curious as to it's purpose. It was adjacent to the small area where the evil, female tyrants lived when they were not tormenting or bullying somebody. I had noticed girls going in and out of the room and I had heard strange noises coming from there. It was actually only a couple of months before my release that I found out what was going on. It was just before Adeleine came to visit and I was able to ascertain from her for definite that my suspicions were correct. And that was tattooing. Girls were sent in there to be 'branded.' Why it never happened to me is another mystery which must remain just that   but I think it was dependent on who had 'rights' to the girl and where their destination was. Whatever the reason I was eternally grateful that I was not scarred to be reminded of my awful ordeal for life.

This may sound a little crazy but I fell into a habit of speaking to what was around me. My world consisted of my room and so the objects in that room became my source of dialogue and meditation. I would deliberately eat my food slowly, digesting each mouthful mindfully, saying things like – "go where you need to go rice and make my body strong." I would speak similarly to my body, to my mind, to my blanket, asking it to keep me warm. Water was definitely limited and I would try and savour each mouthful. I seemed to have a constant thirst and dry mouth so I would ask the water to go into every cell of my body and keep me healthy. I would discipline myself to not have a drink from my water bottle until I had done one hundred exercise moves with it. I am certain all these small actions combined kept me sane.

CHAPTER 17

One day I had my breakfast as I always did and I was pondering how long I had been in this situation. It had been late summer when I first arrived as I knew only too well that we had just come to the end of a second blistering summer. Even though the majority of the time was spent in darkness with no access at all to any natural light, you were strangely aware of whether it was day or night and roughly what season it was. When I first arrived it took me a few months to shake myself out of my zombie state, which was the result of the shock of Sammi's betrayal and being incarcerated, instead of living a free life with his family and sipping coca-cola in an air conditioned house. I remember starting my exercises when it first began to grow colder. It was a great way to keep warm; I would work my body whilst constantly thinking of ways to escape. I tried not to let my imagination roll too far into the world outside my four walls as that was not always healthy but I do truly believe that by doing my exercises it saved my life.

After I realised I had been incarcerated for over two years I fell into a dark place, having the realisation that I had already experienced this sensation of being trapped for two years when I was at Dahagey, then I fell into a depressed stupor which lasted for a long time when I realised that it would be the third year I was entering into. I had managed to make a makeshift seat in the corner of my room as obviously I did not want to sit on my bed. I regarded my seat in the corner as sacred and that is where I spent my spare time. One time a man tried to steer me over to it, I screamed so loud that one of the women came running thinking he was doing something bad to me. The man looked sheepish and ran off and I never saw him again. I often laughed about this as somehow I had won in that situation, I do not know whether he had passed the message on but nobody tried to lure me over to my seat again after that.

I tried to blot out any thoughts about who these men were and why they paid money to do what they did. How could they walk away and wipe their mouths and not have any remorse or compassion over the poor, young girls they left scarred and enslaved? They must get a kick out of keeping their big, dirty secret; but as I say I blotted these thoughts out of my head as much as was humanly possible.

There were some thoughts that went through my head that I found quite destructive. When I thought about my dear Dopo, and the memories I cherished of Papa when I was a little girl, I found the contrast between them and the 'men' I was now experiencing quite horrific. How could they be part of the same species? Every time the 'men' pressed their weight down on me it reminded me of the weight of the water I carried in Dahagey. This was a burden I happily carried because I was doing something good by helping bring fresh water to people in desperate need. This burden I was now experiencing was painful in every way. What did these 'men' achieve by releasing their sperm into innocent, random girls? I felt virtuous by helping provide clean water but what was in the deprived minds of these sick human beings?

Chapter 18

Adeleine had an unusually loud voice and I always heard her approaching, but when she spoke with me she lowered her voice to a beautiful softness that warmed my heart. I have no idea why she singled me out; maybe she saw some strength in me that she didn't see in the other girls. I had a hard, upright chair by the door of my room and here Adeleine would sit whilst I sat on my corner seat. It was very strange at first to be having a calm, "normal" conversation with another human being – one whose eyes oozed compassion and kindness; yet still I struggled to trust her and would sit in relative silence, answering her questions as briefly as possible whilst all the time trying to analyse her.

Inside I wanted to explode, I felt like one of those toys with a spring that you pushed down and then after a little while it sprung up and jumped. Dopo had one, I think it was a giraffe with tall legs and I would giggle for hours waiting for the spring to pop and send my tummy quivering into fits of giggles. Was that me, was that really me - Marna, was I that same little girl, so carefree and untroubled? I remember being an open-eyed, trusting little soul; full of life and expectancy, believing that everyone who came into my path only had my best interests at heart. Now it was so difficult to let my guard down and invite somebody to infiltrate my resilient wall to expose myself enough to a stranger that I would allow myself to confide in them. I kept it all in; I was so scared of being deceived and hurt again. The scars left by what happened with Papa, Sammi and the Rufaros were still very raw, the sores were still weeping.

Adeleine told me about her house and it sounded incredibly beautiful; there was an outdoor area where you could sit and eat and they had a swimming pool with a slide that you could slide down into clean, cool, refreshing bliss. There were windows everywhere and you could look out to the sea and walk to the beach. She explained that her house and garden were never in darkness as she had solar lights everywhere and she liked lighting candles. She made everything sound so real. I would go to sleep and hear the gentle waves splashing against the sand. I remember going to the beach twice when I was a child; it was one of our stopover places when I was in the circus. We would go there in late summer and stay for a couple of weeks. I would get up early and run down to the sandy beach and drink in the beautiful sunrises. I felt like the ocean went on forever and that it all belonged to me; I used to cup my hands and pretend it was all mine. Apart from a few fishermen I had the beach to myself; I would run and do cartwheels and sing and dance. I had so much joy it had to escape; I had to let it out; so much joy – and now? Somehow I had to get over these memories and carry on living, how could this be possible?

This may sound unbelievable, but as I pondered what Adeleine shared with me about her house and garden and surroundings, I realised that I did not know what a solar light was. Also I had never swum in a swimming pool, let alone go down a slide into one. Whether Adeleine was aware of my ignorance or not, I do not know; she probably just thought I was very quiet! When you are not aware that something exists and cannot picture it in your head it is impossible to comment on such phenomena.

Adeleine would visit me twice a week and she tried her hardest to break down my barriers to reassure me that she was on my side and only had my best interests at heart. She seemed to be genuinely distressed every time she witnessed our appalling conditions. I liked her and grew to look forward to her visits. It was such a refreshing change. She showed me photographs of her house and outdoor area with the swimming pool and the beautiful beach and ocean. One even had Benito and Adeleine standing together looking out to the sea; how could that be fake? I asked myself whether it was truly possible that this cheerful, carefree couple could be my saviours. I decided to lay a trap and one day when Adeleine began to gently question my past, I told her a little bit about my acrobat display in the circus. The next time she came to visit I made a point of mentioning the routine, to see whether Adeleine was sincerely interested in me, or whether this was another great hoax that I had stupidly fallen for - yet again.

Adeleine passed the test and remembered my routine – I was so happy! It took a great effort on my part to hold back my relief and excitement. There was hope yet in the human race! A few days later she appeared in my doorway with a serious expression on her face. She told me I needed to make a decision because she and her husband Benito were telling the women captors that they wanted to "buy" me and she could not keep visiting like this for much longer. I did not say much but she left being well aware that I understood the gravity of her message. I felt extremely fearful; it seemed so familiar to the situation when Sammi put pressure on me to make the decision to escape with him. My problem was that my mind had told me that this was the correct thing to do when I agreed to escape with Sammi and everything seemed logical – but how could I possibly trust my judgment now? I hated being put under this pressure and apart from Adeleine I had nobody to confide in or gain confirmation. I enjoyed my conversations with Adeleine but now longed for someone I could sit down with to download all the information I was being presented with, then see whether they agreed with me or not. How could I be sure that Adeleine and Benito were not really just buying me the same way Sammi had?

CHAPTER 19

It was a very scary time. Three years surviving under such horrific conditions was enough to drive the most balanced person crazy; it was an extremely lengthy ordeal. Now I was being asked to make a quick decision based on a few brief meetings with a lady I perceived to be genuine, but who could really know? I had no one to share my thoughts with, and after being imprisoned and not having to think about anything or fend for myself in any way whatsoever, my brain was foggy. I felt as if my brain was a seized up engine and I did not know where to locate the lubricating oil.

Thinking back I recalled seeing Adeleine's husband, Benito, one day when we were having recreation time. It was a couple of months prior to Adeleine's visits and I did not take much notice at the time as there were so many men coming and going; but I do remember that Benito seemed different. He had a look on his face that I had not witnessed in a very long time; looking back I would call the expression 'compassionate.' I remember being aware that his gaze kept resting on me, but not in a sleazy, undressing way that the other men did. It was a respectful look. I used every effort I was able to muster to think back to that day but it was a difficult task. I think our brains go into survival mode when we are challenged with a situation so huge it is beyond our control – whether it be abuse, kidnapping, starvation, being lost or anything where you feel out of your depth – how do you survive? If you constantly dwell on your present circumstances you will become despondent; constantly looking inward and feeling like a victim. Obviously you want to fight with every ounce of your being but if that fight becomes impossible and it is beyond your capabilities to change your circumstances then you have to find an alternative coping strategy. Mine was to do my exercises, try not to think too much about anything and when things became unbearable, I would try to concentrate my thoughts on my happy childhood days.

Now having lived like this for over three years I had the challenge of awakening my thought processes and inner discernment to make a rational decision. The problem I always came back to was that I had made such a gigantic mistake in believing Sammi; how could I possibly trust my instincts now? The other thing that frightened me was that I did not know where the girls went when they left here. What if they went somewhere the same or worse? Nobody spoke of it. One day you would just notice that one of the girls was missing and then invariably a new girl would appear a few days later.

One thing for certain was that I would have to make a decision rapidly. I was petrified and if I didn't make my mind up soon it would make me ill. I found it impossible to eat or sleep with the pressure I was under.

CHAPTER 20

I came to the realisation quite early on in my kidnapping that our captors drugged us. We were given a drink in the evening which must have contained some 'uppers' as it made us jittery and insanely awake all night. Then in the morning we were given a drink which I guessed contained a sedative so that if you didn't actually manage to get any sleep in the daytime you were perpetually dopey. Consequently, given my present predicament and my imminent decision making, I decided to throw my morning drink discreetly away and risk a few sips of the disgusting, dirty water that was offered to us to keep me from dehydration. Apart from the inevitable upset stomach, I quickly ascertained that I was able to think clearer and process the information I was being presented with, as I was now lucid and awake in the daytime hours.

Adeleine came to visit after a few days of my declining the morning cup of dope. I let her talk, discerning (correctly) that this could be her last visit before I had to make the big decision. She began the conversation by telling me how she and Benito had spent the day before. It was hard to take in everything she was saying as my mind was tied in a knot of nerves but what I did digest sounded like a picture of a perfect day if someone had asked you what a perfect day would look like. But could it all be too good to be true?

Then she went on to ask questions about my life at the circus. I wondered why she was interested; she made a comment about me looking strong and I joked and lifted up my sleeve to show her my taut biceps. She gasped and sat back quickly in her chair. I examined my arm to see why she would have such a reaction and noticed the purple welts where I had been tied up in my nightly 'sessions.' I had long since not noticed them. They were on my ankles also and I remember the first time that I saw them I thought – how did they get there? I honestly had no recollection of these torturous events which I am sure in part was due to the drugs, but also my ability to literally switch off and be there in body only; my spirit either was not present or chose to wipe the memory out.

I learnt later it was the latter which was the truth as after a couple of years of recovery the nightmares began – and the healing. The memories had been neatly stored away in a part of my brain but they had not disappeared. I imagined my brain was like a clever, complex computer and had a filing system – things to do, things to do tomorrow and things to be left alone until such a time that the person is capable of dealing with them.

So it was really these two things – Adeleine's reaction on seeing my welts and her genuine interest in my childhood that ultimately made my mind up so I resolved that evening after she left that the decision was firmly cemented in stone and I would leave this appallingly awful dungeon with Adeleine by my side and my head held high. Just before the night time's activities I repeated the mantra – "my name is Marna and I will NEVER give up. I am of sound mind and I am making the correct decision to go with Benito and Adeleine. My life WILL improve and I regret nothing nor hold any bitterness or anger in my heart."

PART THREE
The Emergence Of Weightless Flight

Chapter 21

When you cross the road at a crossroads you have to look in four directions. I thought about this one day when I allowed myself to recall how I ended up being kidnapped and betrayed by the one person I believed to be my true friend. I crossed a road without looking in all four directions. Dahagey was divided up into north, south, east and west and it is so important to look in all four directions before making any decisions. I refused to beat myself up about my mistakes – however the clues were there and staring me right in the face – like a car's headlights that appear suddenly in front of your eyes as you are stunned, thinking – "where did they come from? I did not see them coming at all." I recognise now that much of the problem was that I cogitated the decisions I needed to make with me, myself and I. This was something I determined would not happen again in my lifetime. Maybe we all need to have other people around us as our compass points and if enough people say – "no Marna, you really do not want to head in a northerly direction," then just maybe, I would have listened.

I don't know why but I never mentioned Sammi to the Rufaros. I think that partly I considered him to be my friend and quite relished the idea of having a private companion – big mistake! Also I think I compartmentalised people and activities at Dahagey; I did not mention Sammi to Kali either and she most likely would have sussed him out. She was like that; she was streetwise and took no nonsense from anyone. So these were my mistakes and now I must learn from them. I treasured Eden, it was my reclusive sanctuary and I always thought it was the one positive thing in my endurance at Dahagey - but looking back maybe it was my biggest downfall. I played with the sweet, smiling children because they never challenged me; I could easily hide behind my mask and I took so much pleasure in their company for that very reason. The Rufaros never got to know me either – not really, not the true Marna. Only my family knew her and that carefree, innocent child was long gone. She had now been replaced with a fragile vase that had been smashed

Mary Daniels

into a million tiny pieces. Now the question was – would it be possible to mend the vase and live a meaningful life that was free of pain?

CHAPTER 22

Sitting on a rocking chair on Benito and Adeleine's porch and looking at the sun's rays glistening over the vast ocean made me feel minutely small – yet safe. And feeling safe is a crucial element for maintaining a life that is worthy of living and also a life that is rewarding. Living in perpetual fear, which is the opposite of living in safety, is not in any way conducive to a stable way of living. It can destroy you in a very short space of time. Humans need food, water and shelter to survive and the latter needs to be free from fear in order to thrive. Although I had been diligently exercising for quite a few months prior to my miraculous escape or 'emergence' as I liked to call it, I was very weak and it took me a long time to regain my strength and even longer to even begin to heal from the trauma. Benito jokingly called me 'Kipee,' an abbreviation of kipepeo which means butterfly. I thought it was an amazing achievement that I could even bear to be in the same room as a man, let alone share a joke with one. Of course strictly speaking it wasn't a joke, it was a joyous statement. I smiled at him the first time he called me Kipee but inside I thought, one day I will be a butterfly but right now I am in a cocoon state; I have emerged from being a caterpillar but I still need the protection of the hard-shelled cocoon, and I am in no way ready to spread out my wings and fly quite yet.

Adeleine arranged for their family doctor to visit me one day; she arranged it secretly as she knew that I would freak out if I knew what she was planning. Actually Doctor Mahur was a kind and understanding man. He only asked questions that needed to be asked and was always patient with me. I could tell he knew the basic facts of what I had been through and was horrified by those facts so I did not need to say anything other than that which was absolutely necessary. He took some of my blood but apart from that did not touch me. He did ask whether I had been genitally mutilated in any way – fortunately I had not. The 'customers' in the dungeon got turned on by blood and I always thought it was fortunate that I had heavy periods that lasted quite a number of days as they seemed to be satisfied by that and not demand more blood by cutting me in any way. When we had our recreation times I heard awful stories about broken bottles where glass was left inside girls and infection ensued and it was not uncommon for girls to be unable to physically walk for days on end. I also know that it was not uncommon for girls to die from infections and general lack of hygiene and medical supervision. But the 'customers' got their kicks, the captors got paid and the women jailers turned a blind eye, wiped their mouths and walked back to their whitewashed homes. And as one girl 'disappeared' so you could guarantee another would soon replace. A faceless number in a filthy, dark cell.

The blood tests showed that I was deficient in a number of important vitamins and minerals, especially iron so Doctor Mahur kindly concocted a powder that was mixed in water and I had to hold my nose and drink it three times a day – it tasted bitter and disgusting but as it was digested into my body I was aware of its healing powers, and slowly it became easier for me to rise from my bed in the morning and I felt more energised with each new day. I know that Adeleine and Benito paid for the doctor's fees as well as paying for my escape and my upkeep in their house. I was so grateful yet also felt so unworthy; I tried to help out as much as I could around the house and make myself inconspicuous especially in the evenings, aware that they were a couple and it was their time to relax. Yet very often after dinner they would invite me to sit with them on the porch and they genuinely seemed to enjoy my company. We would play silly card games and talk about nothing in particular and I loved every minute of it!

    Benito was quite a few years older than Adeleine and I later discovered that he had been previously married and had two grown up sons, Adam and Paul, who lived nearby. I found Benito a rather curious person. He was fairly short, yet stocky; not unlike Dopo and he had a face that was full of character. His eyes were small, his nose was decidedly pointed and his teeth were extremely crooked. Adeleine adored him, she was a well-built lady with a serious way about her and I think Benito's cheerful disposition complimented her spells of solemnity remarkably well. I think Adeleine took what was happening to not just me but thousands of other girls very much to heart. I know she went back to the place where I was held after I went to live with her. I would often find her quietly crying. Maybe one day I would be able to help her with her rescue missions, but not right now; it was all too raw so I would gently and silently place my hand upon her shoulder, and we would share a mutual empathy that did not need words.

Although Adeleine was not one to use more words than were necessary she did divulge to me one evening, as we were relaxing on the porch together, what originally motivated her and Benito to get involved in rescuing girls who were enslaved like I was.

The incident happened late one morning as Benito was driving home with Adeleine after a shopping trip. Adeleine saw it first; at first it appeared to be simply a pile of rags discarded at the roadside. Having taken a second glance over her shoulder, Adeleine realised to her horror that the pile of clothes had stick arms and legs protruding out of them.

"Benito, you have to stop – now!" Adeleine screamed.

Benito noticed a highly unusual high-pitched panic in his wife's tone.

"Now, Benito, there's a girl back there, and I think she's dead."

"Really," replied Benito with a touch of frustration. He continued.

"We've all ready trapesed around more shops than we had intended and the meat gets so hot in this car."

"We have to love, we have to. We cannot just leave her rotting away waiting for the jackals to find her."

Benito was all ready reversing the car. As is often the way, it is the woman who first has the initial awakening of an idea, but the man will shortly follow suit, it just takes him a little longer!

Adeleine jumped out of the car and rushed over to the limp, emancipated body. The rags which first caught Adeleine's attention was in fact a filthy, holey summer dress. She could not help but notice that the poor creature had no underwear on and was indeed deceased. Adeleine did not think that she had been there long as the flies had only just begun to find her interesting.

Adeleine turned away and retched, she was not used to the degree of raw, human odour that she now witnessed before her eyes and nose.

"I don't think she has been here long," she said to her husband.

Benito wiped away a tear quickly and replied.

"She is so young, and there is hardly any flesh on her."

Turning to his wife he asked, "do you think she was raped?"

Whilst Benito had been speaking, Adeleine had noticed that there were several purple welts, bruises and cuts on the woman's body. There were a lot that she identified as not being recent, there were many scars. She observed that the areas most affected were her wrists and ankles. It was glaringly obvious that the unfortunate woman had been seized against her will and that this had happened on numerous occasions. So in answering Benito's question she simply stated.

"Yes, my love, she has definitely been raped. My guess would be that she died, and that her captors became frightened and thus threw out of their vehicle. You can actually see tyre marks going across the earth at the side of the road if you look carefully."

Benito agreed. Then the couple agreed on something which I am sure was done on the spur of the moment and in other circumstances would not have been agreed upon; and the situation would have been handled very differently. Whether it was the gnawing thought of the growing temperature of the chicken in the car, or the midday heat, or just an act of impulsion will never be known. The fact was that they were confronted with the enormity of what was in raw reality the scene of a horrendous crime.

The road in which they had been travelling along

was a very quiet one and on this day, at this time it was deserted. To them was given the responsibility of this lonesome, troubled soul.

"Yes, I see the track marks," Benito answered solemnly, before continuing.

"I want to give her a burial, it's the least we can do."

Adeleine sighed as if she was expelling her last breath of air. They both understood how corrupt the police, and authorities in general had become. Although it could be argued that the moral action would have been to notify the police and try and find her family; Adeleine and Benito knew how futile this course of action would be. In reality the rancid corpse would be thrown into the rubbish pit. The police would not have the time or resources to investigate it further. Also Benito and his wife could find themselves the subject of an investigation.

So, taking all things into consideration and acting speedily Benito removed an old blanket from his car. Wrapping the featherlight corpse in it, he found a patch of ground away from the road. He swished a large pile of dirt and leaves to one side. Adeleine and her husband stood hand in hand and solemnly recited the Lord's prayer together. Benito then carefully covered the blanket containing the innocent, forsaken relative of someone – as ultimately we are all related – and bowing their heads they silently made their way home.

This unspoken act of charity was not mentioned

again for months. Then one morning Benito turned to his wife over their breakfast coffee and spoke the words that had been on his mind for a while.

"Do you think anybody could trace that blanket back to me?"

"No, Benito, I do not; it is a very common looking blanket. This country is poor, nobody cares about an old blanket; people are struggling enough just to make ends meet. What I have been thinking about though is the perpetrators of that terrible incident. What if that were the tip of the iceberg? What if this is going on to hundreds of other girls and that one just unfortunately died?"

And so that was to be the beginning of a lifetime's mission. As with all awakenings it begins with a mustard seed.

One morning, after I had been at Benito and Adeleine's house for a few weeks, I was sitting on the porch, having just woken up after yet another sweet sleep, and enjoying a glass of delicious, cold orange juice when Adeleine came home from the shops smiling broadly.

"Morning Marna, did you sleep well?"

"Yes," I smiled back. "I did thank you."

"Well, finish drinking your juice and I then I have a surprise for you."

She sat down and waited for me to finish my juice

– which didn't take long as the feeling of drinking a cold drink out of the fridge was so incredibly gratifying that I never wanted to wait until it warmed up. It was definitely up there on my list of things that I missed at Dahagey and the dungeon where my constant thirst was only slightly abated by the murky, tepid water we were given occasionally. I am not sure how Papa managed it – and I will never find out now – but he had an ingenious way of keeping our food and water cold. I know it involved some special kind of black brick and the bricks had to be kept wet at all times. He called it his 'cooler' and I was often sent to spray water on some material that sort of draped over the top of the device. As a child I thought the cooler was the best thing ever and that Papa was a genius. I idolised everything about him – I guess as a child you have your blinkers on and you only look in one direction. Anyway I would never take a refreshing, cold drink for granted after being deprived of that pleasure for so many years.

As soon as I placed my empty glass on the table Adeleine said I needed to follow her to where she had parked up, so I walked over with her to her jeep. I could see there was a large object in the back but could not make out what it was. Adeleine was silent, she just smiled at me and manoeuvred the mysterious and yet light article from the back of her jeep. Still smiling, she picked it up and carried it round the side of the house to an area of ground just below the porch. Below this patch of ground was a steep slope that went down to the wide, sandy beach. She placed the package on the ground and proceeded to unravel it. As she rolled it out on the ground and flattened it out it suddenly occurred to me what it was. I could not stop the tears from rolling down my cheeks even if I wanted to.

"Oh Adeleine, you bought me a gymnastics mat, that is so kind of you."

I hugged her so hard I could feel her ribs against mine.

"It caught my eye as I was shopping in the market, it isn't new, but I am sure we can clean it up, and isn't this just the perfect spot for it here? I was thinking about where to place it as I was driving home, I couldn't wait to see the look on your face."

"It is so completely perfect I feel as if I am in a dream."

Adeleine laughed.

"My dear child, this is real. This is your home now and this is your reality. Benito and I will do all we can to restore your life to one of safety and happiness and, hopefully in the not too distant future, we will save other poor, wretched girls who through no fault of their own – and I mean that Marna – no - fault - of - your - own – they have ended up locked away and treated worse than animals. Right now Benito is developing some photographs he secretly took at that awful place and hopefully we are going to have an opportunity to speak in meetings to expose the wickedness and horror that is happening literally under our noses. To be able to rescue other girls takes a lot of money. Also, we are just beginning to discover that the gangs who are operating these sex rings are powerful and you have to be careful.

But enough of that talk, let's clean up this mat and see

you practise your acrobatics!"

CHAPTER 23

At last I had a reason to wake up in the morning! I would practise my gymnastics early in the morning, before breakfast; then as the bright, yellow sun began her ascent into the deep, blue sky it would be too uncomfortable to exercise so I would sit in the shade and read or sew. I was trying to embroider a cushion, it was coming on slowly but I enjoyed working on it, it was a distraction. Then I would often enjoy the wonderful sensation of sliding into the clear water of the swimming pool. I was trying to teach myself to swim but it wasn't easy! Also I was very body conscious and wore long shorts when I was performing on my gymnastics mat; but they weren't really suitable for swimming! In the fading light of late afternoon I would continue practising my moves until the sun turned deep red. What joy filled my heart – but oh how I ached! I tried to help out as much as I could around the house. I would sweep the yard every morning and evening and do the washing up whenever it needed doing. I was always aware that I was a guest and never wanted to take this huge, miraculous privilege for granted.

Sometimes I would wake in the middle of the night and be in a cold sweat and most of the time my recurrent oh-too-real dream was that I was being forced to enter a vehicle against my will and as I hid under a blanket I would wake up shivering with fear. I would carefully switch my bedside lamp on until after quite a while I felt safe enough to move. Strangely enough I could not get to sleep with a light on, maybe I was so used to the darkened atmosphere where I was held. My eyes really struggled with the bright sunlight when Benito and Adeleine first rescued me. Adeleine kindly bought me some sunglasses. They were the first things she handed to me as we emerged from that awful place. In another situation I would have found it funny that of all things she felt necessary to bring me she would hand me a pair of sunglasses. But Adeleine was like that, she was very perceptive; when she gave you eye contact you felt as if she looked right into your very soul – I was extremely grateful for the shades and I wore them constantly for the first few days of freedom.

Benito joked with me when I had my shades on and called me 'Stevie!' It was years later when I happened to see a video of Stevie Wonder and realised why he called me Stevie. At the time the comment passed right over my head. I had been in a concealed cocoon and not aware of anything much other than keeping safe and out of danger's way for a very long time. I had missed many years of learning the things that you do naturally as you travel along in life. Most people have somebody walking beside them to show them the way and I was only too aware of my ignorance and lack of general knowledge. I felt like a plant that had being thriving, then was placed in a dark room with little water so that as it emerged into the daylight it's growth was stunted and it was much smaller and weaker than the other plants that had been allowed to grow in a healthy environment. But I did not succumb to self-pity – far from it – we would often laugh about certain situations or things I had no idea about!

The morning that Benito and Adeleine came to fetch me I could not stop vomiting. Every time I thought about leaving with strangers and getting into an unknown car made my stomach expel its contents. I was surprised to see Benito with Adeleine as I had assumed she would be on her own as she had been visiting me alone, but I think in their wisdom they thought it wiser to come together. There is strength in numbers and if there was any trouble then it is always preferable to have a man present in these circumstances. It didn't help the situation that the escape took place in the early morning so the resemblance to my departure at Dahagey was not lost on me. Back then I had been so excited about going to live with Sammi's family in their lovely house with air conditioning and ice cold cola. Now I had heard about slides leading into swimming pools and a porch that looked out to the ocean.

No, this was different, it had to be. In the end I rationalised my thinking into – "well whatever happens I will leave this dungeon and I will not be succumbed to daily rapes, torture and starvation, whatever the outcome it has to be an improvement." And with that mind-set I managed to calm my nerves enough to be able to walk out of that long corridor, supported each side by the dear couple who left the comfort of their affluence and paid with their hard earned money to help me walk towards the light – literally – at the end of the tunnel and support me in rebuilding my life.

CHAPTER 24

Benito worked at a local garage and he was the manager there. The word 'manage' seemed to keep occurring in my circle and as I sat on the porch one day I thought about what the word manage means. We manage our lives to the best of our ability and if we are not managing then we certainly know about it! But if we are not aware that we are not managing then people around us most assuredly are. I guess another word for manage is 'cope'; so Benito copes with his garage and the employees that work for him and he is able to deal with everything that is involved with the business.

I am managing and I have been managing my life throughout the whole ordeal and although there have been times when I have very nearly fallen under the momentous weight that I was carrying I have managed to stay afloat. I think there are two reasons that can be credited for this although I believe we all have a basic personality to work with initially. The first reason I did manage I would say is that I tried to be kind to myself and to be grateful for small things. I think this was in my make up anyway but certainly Ummi Rufaro helped in that area. The second reason is that I tried to look after myself as best as I could and work with the environment by which I was limited at the time. I think these two things kept me afloat. I saw many girls in my three years of dungeon living go under. To start off with they appeared very serious and wouldn't know a joke if it hit them on the nose! They soon lost motivation and became lethargic; I am not criticising them, it was desperately sad to watch them slip away. As I have said before I had to utilise my energies and, if I allowed myself to get involved with these girls and befriend them and give them some advice, it would have been detrimental on my health. They could all too easily have drained me of whatever little resources I possessed.

I did retreat into my own cocoon deliberately not speaking to anyone and although this would not be a healthy way of living in the long term I believe that for that time this was the wisest solution. Anyway it must have worked because I was sitting on a porch surrounded by love and security and was in my own mind – managing!

Another thing I discovered was important was to take one day at a time. When you have suffered a trauma a twenty four hour day can become a very short space of time. It takes a long time to heal from any kind of trauma; whether it is shock or death or any trauma it is a long healing process. Even a week can pass quickly, then months go by until you finally realise that you are healing and you are finding everyday situations easier and less stressful than you did a while back. Also you come to the awareness that you are not constantly focusing on the trauma or effects of it and that you are not persistently pushing aside the nagging dark thoughts that rise

Mary Daniels

up from somewhere on the inside of you. Whereas at one time those thoughts were like a huge mountain of black coal, now it was more like a termite hill and everyone can manage a termite hill, can't they?

CHAPTER 25

Sunday at Benito and Adeleine's house was a family day and we often went to the beach. Benito had two sons from his previous marriage, Adam who lived over a hundred miles away and worked repairing railway lines, and a younger son Paul who lived nearby. So Paul often joined us for our Sunday family days. He had the same gentle disposition as Benito and I felt reasonably comfortable around him. He was slightly taller than his father with the same unkempt, wavy hair which almost had a life of its own. He would come to the house occasionally but was always quiet and rather timid. One day as I was practising on my gymnastics mat I was conscious of him watching me. I stole him a glance, sensing he had something to say and, knowing he was a man of few words, I paused.

"I could flatten the earth underneath your mat if you like?"

"Oh that would be great, it may look flat but my bruises tell me otherwise."

My laugh was not reciprocated and Paul flattened

the earth a few days later. He did a great job and even put some matting made from old tyres around the sides of the mat. I enjoyed watching him work, he was very dexterous with his hands and he never seemed to rush. The art of conversation was definitely not his strong point though! He reminded me of a heavy hardback book that takes a lot of effort to open and when you do, you notice the print is tiny and difficult to decipher with absolutely no pictures. You know that if you take the time to read the book the story will be fascinating but it will take a lot of exertion to find the energy to study the text.

Paul unquestionably had secrets and would often sit with a faraway look in his eyes but he was a kind man and I noticed that he distracted me from my inner demons when he was around. We had pleasant family Sundays together on the beach. The sea looked so inviting and I longed to dive in. I ventured a paddle but it was not the same. I was incredibly conscious of my body, especially around Benito and Paul. After a few weeks of me taking a sedate paddle whilst everyone else had a whale of a time splashing about in the waves Adeleine did the sweetest thing. She bought me a beautiful, sparkling leotard that could double up as a swimsuit. It was a bright, turquoise colour with silver, sparkling threads worked through it. It had a skirt that covered my thighs and it went quite high up my chest so I felt comfortable wearing it. It also had wide shoulders; it was so kind of her to be so thoughtful and kind to me and the following Sunday it felt amazing to feel the salty water envelop me. I felt weightless as I floated with the waves washing over me and the warmth of the sun penetrating my very being.

I began going down to the sea early in the morning and jumping in the water. It was so refreshing and since Doctor Mahur had supplied me with the nutrients my body had lacked and Adeleine had been feeding me up with her wonderful cuisine, my strength was gradually returning. I looked forward to these early morning swims and I would savour the sweet morning air as I ran down to the sea shore. I think it is not until something is taken away from you that you fully appreciate it, whether it's sight or hearing or in my case fresh air and daylight. I would never take for granted the spotless blue sky, the still freshness of a new day and the sheer fact that I was alive.

One afternoon, as I was practising on my gymnastics mat a car pulled up and I would later discover that the young man who alighted was in fact Paul's older brother, Adam. He looked different to Benito and Paul; he was much taller and stockier of build. He wore his hair extremely short but it suited him. He had quite a chiselled look about him but he seemed friendly. I was soon to understand that this was not just a social call but that Adam in fact had several issues going on in his increasingly complicated life.

Adam lived in a large town one hundred and twenty miles away. He worked trying to fix a dilapidated railway line. He was married with three young daughters but as the tale began to unravel I discovered that he had another woman on the go and that she was now pregnant – what a mess! Here was one son living the simplest, minimalistic life you could imagine; Paul lived frugally in a hut on a derelict piece of ground. Then there was this other son in an increasingly complicated and complex situation.

Being on the outside, as I was, I found it thought-provoking the different ways in which Benito and Adeleine reacted to Adam's news. Adeleine was horrified to hear that Adam had made another woman pregnant and on top of everything else it appeared that Adam had large debts and financial commitments which he was not able to honour. As I sat on the porch in a lovely shady area, gently rocking on a rocking chair with a refreshing cold glass of juice in my hand. the recurring thought entered my mind that I would never take my freedom and simple life for granted – ever! And I made a vow to myself that whatever the future held I would determine as much as was humanly possible to keep my life free of complications and stress.

Benito, on the other hand seemed to think that it was not Adam's fault that he was in this predicament. He argued that Adam was a man and that it was difficult to be married to a wife who was constantly tired, looking after three young children who were born close together and that it was only natural that Adam should stray and seek release elsewhere. It made me sad to witness these conversations as it started to cause friction between Benito and Adeleine and as, always in these situations it was hard for Adeleine as Adam was not her son and I got the feeling that she would have dearly loved for her and Benito to have had a child of their own. Once Adam went back home to his home the atmosphere lightened and I think Benito and Adeleine settled the matter by not bringing the subject up.

Marna

I called it the 'A saga.' Not out loud but when I thought about these things. My upbringing was a sheltered one; all I knew was the close knit family of the circus. I never ventured out without a chaperone and I never witnessed another family up close. Occasionally I would overhear some people talking as they waited to enter the big tent and I remember hearing a couple of domestic arguments but this 'A saga' was fascinating for me to be privy to; to be part of something up close which seemed so foreign to me.

I did feel sorry for Adam, he seemed pleasant enough; he just reminded me of a whirlwind that was blown along by an unknown force causing havoc yet not aware of its strength and destructive nature. I am sure he never meant to hurt anyone – but he had and the repercussions would be enormous. A couple of weeks after he visited and caused havoc in his wake Benito decided to travel and stay with him for a while and try and help him sort things out. I noticed that Paul strategically kept out of the way when Adam was here. He showed his face one evening but didn't even stay long enough to sit down before making his excuses and leaving. I didn't blame him, these emotional issues can be draining and have a way of affecting everything; but I was aware that Paul obviously was hiding something and I wondered whether he had suffered some emotional upset in the past and thus felt unable to cope with the 'A saga.' Certainly there seemed to be an understanding between him and his Papa and Adeleine and they did not pressurise him when he made his rather abrupt exit.

I did not spend too much time pondering Adam's predicament but it did make me question things somewhat. Why was it perceived to be different for a man to 'need' sex in a way that was almost an outside force driving them and that the force was out of their control? Yet if a woman fell pregnant out of a respectful situation it was totally frowned upon and she was made to feel she had done a terrible thing. I was young yet had enough understanding to guess that this was true for the vast majority of cultures. Do women have the same drive as a man? It takes both a seed and a sperm to create life which ultimately is what sex is created for, and the sex drive is to make sure a new generation is produced. Adam already had three daughters; why couldn't he be content with them and his wife? I had seen photographs of them all together and they looked lovely, a really happy family.

Surely everything made a huge difference when you were married. The two families combined and you worked as a team. Why couldn't Adam work as a team with his wife instead of seeking solace elsewhere? I know that Adeleine had a faith and that her opinion was that marriage is sacred and you do not violate the vows you made to one another. I was philosophical about the whole situation and thought that just that one moment of temptation had now caused so much heartache, especially as there were three innocent lives involved.

CHAPTER 26

I was becoming increasingly aware that I was looking forward to Paul's visits more and more and if he didn't call round one day, I missed him. He had a dog called 'Charmer,' a scruffy looking black and white mongrel that looked like he constantly needed a brush. He was a lovely dog and had a way about him that charmed everyone in his midst, hence the name. Invariably I would hear Charmer approaching before I was aware of Paul's presence and he would bound up to me and no matter what I was doing he would lick his greeting. Paul would smile and I aware of having a tingling sensation which was a new experience for me. It was like being awakened to something inside that I was not aware was dead – or places that were in me I did not know existed. I was in two minds whether I enjoyed this new awareness; it had a way of consuming my every waking – and sleeping - moment. I found the whole experience totally overwhelming – exciting and exhilarating and I felt alive. Yes alive, that is what it made me feel and I was loving it. When I thought about Paul I felt like the sky was the limit - my jumps were higher, my leaps were longer and my cartwheels straighter!

I liked the fact that Paul was not a talker; there

was nothing worse than someone endlessly asking you questions. I was neither ready nor prepared for that. Adam was insistent that Benito had taken him and Paul to the circus when they were young boys and he said he remembered seeing me there. His story sounded authentic enough. He got my name right and he described the act that Zena and I performed where we each jumped through a huge hoop simultaneously as they crisscrossed high across the roof of the marquee and then the hoops were set on fire to huge "oohs and ahhs" followed by applause from the audience. Oh how I loved performing that routine with Zena, I wonder whether it would ever be possible to have that telepathy with another soul – I doubt it. Zena and I did not need words.

I approached the subject with Paul early one evening after I had been practising for the day. We were sitting on the porch on chairs at right angles with each other.

"So what do you think? Have I improved since I was a little girl?"

Paul frowned so I went on.

"Adam remembers when Benito took him and you to the circus and he remembers seeing me, (I threw my arms theatrically in the air,) 'the one and only magnificent Marna!' He remembered the burning hoop that I leaped through."

Well I don't know what reaction I was expecting but Paul surprised me. He keep his eyes firmly fixed to the ground as I was speaking and then abruptly got up from his seat and silently walked away leaving his drink – and me. I decided it was probably wise to let sleeping dogs lie as the saying goes and I didn't bring the subject up again.

Paul definitely intrigued me; I had not been to his house come shack but I had heard enough descriptions to picture it in my head clearly enough. There was no electricity for a start, Paul cooked on a gas stove and as far as I knew used candles for lighting. The question was, was he happy? Was this way of living his choice or was he simply running away from whatever was haunting him? Some people I know do choose this way of life but the more I got to know Paul I was convinced in his case it was the latter and that there were an awful lot of things he was escaping from.

It is difficult, nigh on impossible to form an acquaintance with somebody who a) is a closed book and b) actually does not do that much with his life and therefore does not have an awful lot to say. After my aborted attempt at having a conversation about the past, even my past in the circus, I recognised that reminiscing was now a non-starter. He always joined us for our Sunday beach days – I suspected it was mainly for Adeleine's superb picnics which she often spent all day Saturday preparing. I enjoyed his company, it never elevated to anything higher than laughing at Charmer's antics or admiring Adeleine's cooking skills but that was probably what I needed anyway. I doubtless wasn't ready for an in depth discussion, I was still healing. But was Paul? Was he healing or had he ever attempted to begin the healing process.

As much as Benito and also Adeleine were clearly fond of Paul I sensed that they found him somewhat frustrating at times. I remember one time after I had been staying with Benito and Adeleine for about three months, Adeleine tripped over a loose stone and sprained her ankle. Also at this time they were both going to the dungeon quite a lot. This was never discussed in front of me to the point that they either went silent or immediately changed the subject as soon as I came into their vicinity. I knew when they went there because it was a three hour car journey both ways and there was nowhere else that they went that took that long. I also suspected that they were helping another unfortunate soul to leave. When they went on their trips I wondered whether they would bring a girl back here. Paul came round when Adeleine was obviously in pain with her ankle and stressed and tired about whatever they were doing at the dungeon, and he came into the kitchen and sat down on a stool that was by the counter.

"Do you have anything I can clean a burnt saucepan with? I burnt some cheese in it last night."

"Hmm," I thought to myself; if somebody had come into my kitchen and asked me for something without even asking how I was I would definitely not be happy and I perceived that Adeleine was not at all impressed with his manners. She remained quiet for a while and I was interested to hear how she would react.

She spoke in a controlled, calm voice.

"Paul, do you remember a couple of weeks ago I asked you if you could be so kind to move the loose stones that were on the path outside the front door where we walk to get to the car?"

"Yeah sorry Adeleine, I didn't get around to it."

"Well because you 'didn't get around to it' I tripped over a loose stone this morning as I was walking to the car and have sprained my ankle, it will take up to six weeks to heal."

Paul shot me a shy, embarrassed look but did not speak. I wanted to give him a big shake and fix what it was that was broken in him. Adeleine eventually broke the awkward silence. She sighed and motioned to me.

"Marna dear, would you be a love and make us all some tea? I am going to rest my ankle."

She spoke the last sentence deliberately, stealing a glance at Paul, clearing showing her frustration and annoyance.

So the three of us sat down to a subdued cup of tea. Charmer came bounding up after a while and I was so pleased to see him; I felt like a kettle had just boiled and broken the tangible tension.

Chapter 27

On the whole Adeleine was a private person. She went about her work with a quiet, industrious steadfastness; always having a smile on her face and a listening ear for anyone who came into her vicinity yet was happy in her own space. My respect for her grew with each passing day with the fact that she not only welcomed me into her family home, but also made me feel valued and genuinely wanted. I was aware that her number one consuming thought was how she could help the kidnapped girls and, in order to obtain awareness and maximum support, it was necessary to publicise the situation - but because Adeleine treasured her privacy there were not many people that she met on a regular basis. Also she had to be careful as obviously there was an element of danger as the gangs involved did not want their lucrative business exposed. Adeleine spoke briefly to me about this matter, I think I was her ' thought bouncer' and as she bounced her thoughts off to me, I listened, and if I felt I could add anything I would answer; if not I just listened.

We were now entering the ferocious heat of summer and after a busy morning and lazy lunch Adeleine and I would swing gently on the swing seats in a shady spot of the porch. Occasionally we slept; sometimes we read and sometimes we just swung - both absorbed in our private meditations but we very rarely talked. One afternoon we were swinging as usual. I could tell at lunch that there was something pressing on her mind; she ate slowly and contemplatively and we enjoyed our food in relative silence. After our lunch had settled and we had had a nice rest Adeleine enlightened me with her thoughts.

"We have to be discreet….." She began.

I nodded, having an inkling of where this conversation was going.

"…..We can't just go in all guns blazing but we need

help Marna, and we need people to get on board with us. Even for Benito and I to help just one girl takes time – as you well know. And all the while we are dedicating our time in saving one life hundreds more are being caught and are suffering. Also we have spent hours securing the release of a girl and then at the last minute she gets cold feet – as you nearly did – and refuses our help. It is time consuming and costly."

I do not think I had properly digested what it took for Benito and Adeleine to step in and help me before. Obviously I appreciated all they did but I had not completely absorbed it – the hundreds of miles travelling to and fro to visit me – just me – not to mention the 'price' they paid for my release. Oh the eternal gratitude that I felt could never be put into words.

But there were hundreds of girls that we knew about – and thousands we didn't being held in the same filthy, disgusting underground holes. And these living souls had no one – no one in the world that not only could fight for them but that were even aware of their existence and desperate heartache. No wonder Adeleine was often found lost in her thoughts; the enormity of the situation simply overwhelming her. I often wished that I had more compassion for the girls I inwardly said good bye to that infamous day when I walked into the incredibly bright sunlight in my shades. I think if I had stayed there much longer my lack of empathy with the mainly apathetic, resigned zombies which the girls became would have turned into detestation and that would not have been healthy for either party. I think that because I was trying so very hard to rise above the appalling conditions and to do something, even if that something was just to do a few bicep curls it was more than my counterparts were doing. But I never got to know any of them; for the majority I never learned their names and I did not know their stories – and we certainly all have a story. I did not fully appreciate their struggles and inner sufferings. Now I was free and living a dream-filled life but was made acutely aware each day of the horrifying reality that was these poor creature's enduring, endless days.

"So I thought we would have a party!" Announced Adeleine to my complete surprise which certainly shocked me out of my contemplations! I imagined she was planning a quiet fundraising talk!

It was decided that the party would be held in two weeks' time. We printed out a hundred invitations and I thought that two weeks would give us plenty of time to arrange everything. But I had totally underestimated how much work was involved in arranging a social event – there was so much to do!

I had nothing but utter respect for Adeleine. Here was a woman who was not naturally a sociable person and yet she was stepping out of her comfort zone for the sake of waifs and strays that she did not know personally and they may not even thank her. She had only just recovered from her fall and yet was doing all this for them – for me.

I have never done so much baking in my life! I could feel my biceps strengthen daily. First we made two large fruit cakes and then we stored them in tins to be iced and decorated the day before the party. We made potato salads, rice salads and fruit salads – so much chopping! Benito brought two chickens and Paul brought two large fish that he had caught from a local pond. At least he contributed something I thought to myself. On the day of the party Adeleine and I awoke early and baked bread rolls. I loved the aroma of the yeast rising and it was so peaceful to share the kitchen with Adeleine in the early hours of the morning whilst most people were still asleep.

We decided to make a huge bowl of punch and as we were waiting for the dough to rise we set about washing and cutting up some strawberries, grapes and oranges.

"Do you think Paul will come this afternoon?" I asked Adeleine.

"Only I've noticed that he hasn't been around much whilst we've been preparing everything."

"Too much like hard work!" Adeleine laughed.

"Do you think he's lazy then?"

"I don't know child; there is a lot of baggage in that boy's head and I think it weighs him down. No, he isn't lazy and I shouldn't have said that and no, I very much doubt that he will make an appearance at the party later. I know you like him Marna, I see the way you look at him; you probably recognise a wounded soul and it warms my heart to see that you are able to be comfortable around him. You have opened up and allowed yourself to begin the healing journey but Paul hasn't even stepped onto the starting block."

She looked at me to see if I shared the joke but my head was down; I was concentrating on cutting up the fruit, taking in every syllable of the information that she was divulging. It was the first time that either she or Benito had said anything of length about Paul. I had either been part of or overheard plenty of conversations regarding Adam but somehow Paul was just a sad, lonely figure on the side line. The sight of Paul wandering in and out of an all too familiar state of noncommittal just seemed to be the norm and if they didn't see him for a few days then 'that was just Paul.' But why? As time went on I felt an almost unrelenting compulsion to discover Paul's secret but it would take a few more days before I did unravel the onion layers. Right now we had a party to get ready!

Chapter 28

We decorated the porch with colourful streamers; we had a table in the middle containing the punch and four large, oblong tables with the food on around the sides. All the porch area was decorated brightly. I was so proud of Adeleine and my achievements. I couldn't believe there had been no disasters. I had never made anything like this lovely food before, it all seemed so complicated and so many skills and steps to remember; I absolutely marvelled at Adeleine's skill and patience with me.

I sensed that she was rather concerned about how many people would respond to our invitations. In the end there was a steady trickle of people appearing throughout the afternoon but nothing spectacular. Mostly they were neighbours or acquaintances known through Benito's garage and I did not sense that any were short of money. As soon as they started arriving I felt incredibly awkward and shy; the whole experience made me realise how completely socially inept I was. It highlighted my stunted adolescent development. I tried to help out quietly in the background, keeping one eye on Adeleine in case she needed me. Benito was there all afternoon and was actually brilliant. Whenever I caught a snippet of a conversation my emotion was one of immense sadness. This is a typical response to Adeleine and Benito's heartfelt pleas of help:

"Oh it is such a terrible thing that is happening and I would love to help but I am just so busy (with whatever) at the moment otherwise I would willingly offer you support – but here, have this."

And with that Benito and Adeleine were presented with a cheque. Two minutes of someone's precious time taken up and don't ask for anymore.

The 'party' finished as soon as it started and everyone drifted away. I felt utterly deflated and I am sure Adeleine did too. Benito had given a lady a lift home and Adeleine was in the kitchen. I brought in the last of the dishes from the porch. I looked around the kitchen and it looked like a huge amount of work was needed to tidy everything up. What a lot of work for a couple of cheques I thought. I didn't know where to begin. I started to half-heartedly potter about; Adeleine looked as if she was about to collapse. Our gazes met and brushing her hair with her hand she said-

"Stop child; just stop; this can all wait until tomorrow."

I was clearing up the glasses we used for the punch; there was a little bit left at the bottom of the bowl and Adeleine poured two glasses and said –

"Let's take these on the porch and I'll tell you about Paul; I noticed that your thoughts were drifting in his direction after we spoke earlier, I hope you weren't expecting him to attend the party this afternoon, were you?"

"No, I wasn't, I knew he wouldn't come but I am intrigued as to why he behaves the way he does."

"Then come Marna dear; we will sit awhile and switch off from the uninspiring afternoon that we have both endured."

It was a beautiful, sultry, calm evening and I sat back and encouraged Adeleine to continue.

"Benito and his former wife had three children; there were Adam, the eldest, Paul and a sister called Maria who was three years younger than Paul. Paul was twelve years old and Maria nine when one afternoon they were alone in the house and there was a fire. I don't know the full details but Paul managed to escape from the house and from what I understand he absolutely tried his hardest to rescue Maria but the roof rafters collapsed and she was trapped underneath. As much as the firelighters assured Paul that there was nothing more he could have done and it was just a terrible accident he could not shake off the feelings of guilt and has not been able to since. It is desperately sad but apparently he was very close to Maria and from what I have heard she was quite a character. I have seen a few photographs and she was a tiny little thing but had strength a hundred times mightier than her size. She was a tom boy and a huge part of Paul's life.

Benito tried everything to help Paul get over his heartache but obviously he was grieving too. He wanted to try for another child but his wife did not want to and would not let Benito near her and it ultimately led to the break-up of their marriage. Benito wanted them all to go to family counselling but Paul refused. Twelve is a difficult age at the best of times but after a while as Paul remained in his shell Benito and Adam came to the conclusion that this was the way it was going to be. Paul began to spend more and more time away from home and would stay in the woods for days on end, eventually building the shack where he has been living for the last eight years or so. I am not sure if he finished his schooling; as you know Marna it is not easy to have a conversation with him and Benito is not much better to be honest. The memory of Maria has been bottled up and sealed securely. Paul believes that if he stays in his cocoon he is safe and does not need to deal with any issues that are crippling him. A couple of weeks ago Benito and I spoke to a girl being held in the caves and it transpired that her name was Maria. It was like a thunder bolt had fallen on Benito's head, I saw him almost physically crumble. I have only been with Benito for six years so I am not privy to everything that happened before then and nobody truly knows a man's private thoughts, as you yourself

Mary Daniels

understand only too well, don't you my dear child. Only God above is entrusted to our innermost sanctuary for He knows every one of our fears and hopes and desires."

CHAPTER 29

I was grateful to Adeleine sharing what she did; it helped me to make sense of a curious, lonely man who I was conscious of having growing affections for. Paul came round the following afternoon; I was tempted to say – "yes Paul, all the work is finished, it is safe for you to visit" I resisted the urge but I felt like a light had shone into the situation. Not only did I empathise with his intangible grief but I completely understood his decision that the best way of dealing with it was to totally shut himself away and have as little involvement with the outside world as possible.

I was sitting cross-legged on my mat, not doing anything much when Charmer came bounding up, followed by Paul. He was smiling, I half-heartedly returned the sentiment.

"I know it's not exactly the afternoon that you and Adeleine wanted but at least you got a couple of healthy cheques out of all your effort."

"Yes, that is as may be but it was a huge amount of effort to be met by stony indifference for the most part.

My muscles ache more than if I had done a back to back gymnastics routine!"

"Well the party is over now and there is no point dwelling on it or being hard on yourselves; maybe the exercise did you good!"

He managed to dodge a cushion that I playfully threw at him. It was a blistering hot day and I had a sudden desire to run down to the beach – so that is what I did! Charmer thought it great fun and swiftly followed with Paul bringing up the rear. I took off my sandals and splashed in the calm, refreshing spray. Paul joined me and it felt so incredibly invigorating to pull my head back and laugh out loud. I do not think I had realised how tense and sombre the last couple of weeks had been. Adeleine and I had been so excited about our fundraising day; only to be left with a deflated hole in our stomachs when it was all over. And I think I had been carrying the weight of Adeleine's anguish on my shoulders as I felt so sorry for her. My emotions as always were mixed with the eternal appreciation I had for her and Benito and my total inability to ever repay them.

Paul and I sat on the beach and dried off; by the time we headed back to the house Adeleine was a bit cross, wondering where we had been for so long. I found it sweet that she cared, the question was - did Paul care about me or was he just using me as a distraction? As we lazed on the golden sand life seemed to stand still and everything seemed so perfect. What would have made it complete perfection would have been if this mysterious enigma of a man sitting next to me had looked me in the eyes as we talked and slowly turned and kissed me. I lingered as long as I could manage but I knew Adeleine would have the supper ready and the last thing I wanted was to disappoint her.

We ate supper in comparative silence. Adeleine had made a simple chicken and rice dish which was delicious but I found it hard to physically swallow. My appetite had disappeared and I was having a problem putting food into my mouth when it felt like there was a blockage in my throat. I couldn't bear the formality of sitting around a table eating a meal when the tension in the air felt tangible. There were so many huge, intense discussions that were needed in order to clear the air and I knew that Adeleine would sit on the porch afterwards as was our custom and that she would want a conversation with me about the afternoon's events and I just couldn't stomach it - literally.

"Thank-you Adeleine, that was a lovely meal but I have a headache coming on, please may I be excused?"

She gave me one of her 'knowing looks.'

"Yes, go and I will see you in the morning."

Which translated meant – "you're not getting away with it that easily my girl. we will talk tomorrow, of that you can count on."

The following morning I arose to the unusual

sound of raised voices. I waited until I could hear the voices fade away, then I stood up and drew the curtains. As I did so I saw Benito hurriedly driving off in his car. I went down to breakfast.

"Where has Benito gone?" I asked Adeleine but before she answered I noticed her wiping her nose on her apron. She turned to face me.

"He has gone to visit Adam, trying to sort out his mess and just leaving me on my own to sort out ours."

I touched her arm affectionately.

"You have me, you are not here alone. I will make us some coffee."

Poor Adeleine, sometimes it seemed she had the weight of the world on her shoulders. I let her speak, I felt that if she poured out her heart to me she would feel lighter; we all need that feeling and often do not realise how much we need to unload until we do not have the opportunity, for whatever reason and the burden remains a heavy stone, locked up inside our silent souls. I made our coffee and we sat at the big, wooden table. Adeleine started to speak.

"After you retired to bed last night I went out to the porch as you know is my custom. Paul joined me and asked when Benito was coming home as he was working late at the garage. I said he wouldn't be long and that he was welcome to wait. We relaxed for a while and spoke about small things and then Paul started to become rather impatient, you know how he misses his shack after a while?"

I laughed, picturing the scene; Adeleine continued.

""Paul shuffled his feet and asked - maybe you could be so kind as to pass a message on to Benito? I said - of course, what do you want to say to him? Paul said – "well I know he is going to visit Adam tomorrow and I was wondering if he could pop into the bureau and see if he can get a copy of my birth certificate?" He fumbled in his pocket and handed me a banknote and standing up said – "that should cover it." He started to walk off but I called out to him. I said -

"Hang on a minute Paul, it's not a problem, I am sure Benito won't mind going to the bureau although this is actually the first that I have heard about his planned jaunt tomorrow. It is not the greatest timing if I am honest and I am just wondering what you want your birth certificate for?"

And do you know how he answered me Marna?""

I couldn't think why Paul would need his birth certificate so I shook my head.

""Well he turned round pensively and whispered shyly – "because I want to ask Marna to marry me!""

I placed my coffee cup on the kitchen table, afraid

that I might spill it as I suddenly felt shaky.

"Well that answers your question about whether he feels the same way about you as you obviously do about him, doesn't it? Paul is a good man Marna, he has a pure heart, he's just not that great at showing his emotions! I thought that I would share our conversation with you as it will give you some time to evaluate what you want to say when he pops the question! I am sure Benito will be able to secure his birth certificate, they are all held in the bureau. Obviously all their original documents were destroyed in the fire that killed Maria. I think Benito will only be gone for a few days; especially as I made my feelings very well known this morning about him leaving so suddenly when there is so much to do. We were supposed to be going to collect another girl tomorrow and you know that there is only a short window of opportunity to carry out these missions Marna."

I did know that – I knew that only too well. This was an awful lot to take in and definitely not the conversation I had envisioned we would be having over our morning coffee!

CHAPTER 30

I didn't know what to do with myself, it didn't make any difference how I tried to occupy my time I still had constant butterflies fluttering about inside of me. Paul did not appear at the house for a couple of days and when he did pop over he seemed awkward and I even noticed him blush as he looked at me! His emotional life had been so stunted, he had been existing, putting everything on hold – and now I came along! He was in his early twenties but really he was still a young boy. I overheard a conversation one day with him and Adeleine. Adeleine had been spending time with a girl called JD at the dungeon and time was running out to release her. Benito was with Adam and so he could not help her as he usually did. Adeleine had gained her confidence and didn't want all that hard work to go to waste. So she approached Paul and I was surprised - and secretly impressed that he was willing to accompany her and help to release JD and put himself on the line. I wondered how deep Paul's understanding was about what went on at the dungeon. Was he being brave or simply naïve? If the former then just maybe he was suitable husband material after all!

I thought about the subject of marriage a lot over

the next few days. Apart from Paul's obvious issues, was I ready to be intimate with someone? When I was in Paul's company I was certain that I was, but was I? Also did I want to be beholden to another human being so soon as I had discovered my freedom? So many questions and I wasn't sure where to look for the answers. I definitely wanted to be Paul's wife, I loved him and that was never in doubt. The question of whether he was sufficiently healed enough and prepared to let me into his world was a question I wondered about.

It seemed to me that we were both in a strange time warp. I had been staying with Benito and Adeleine for nearly four months and summer would soon be coming to an end. Was this the end of my season here? It had been a truly wonderful time and I would never forget it but I could not spend the rest of my life doing cartwheels and washing up forever.

Paul went to the dungeon with Adeleine and they came home with JD. Oh how I struggled with her! I found myself with an extremely limited supply of patience when I was around her. She seemed so pathetic and every time she asked Adeleine for something it annoyed me because she was quite capable of figuring things out herself if she simply applied herself. I just saw her as a burden and it upset me to see how drained Adeleine looked with the extra work she created. I understood how much JD had suffered but I felt like she did not help herself and seemed almost to revel in her victimhood and self-pity. I was constantly telling her to come and help do the chores but she was so incredibly slow and weak she was no help at all. She spent the majority of her time in her room which

I was unkindly glad about; but how was that helping her? Doctor Mahur came to visit her as he did me and told her she needed the vitamin D that was found in sunlight. His advice was costing Benito and Adeleine money but did she care? Would she listen?

    I sat on the beach at dusk and beat myself up about how uncharitable my thoughts towards JD were. I came to the conclusion that the very thought of her was not healthy for my personal growth and it was best that I just kept out of her way as much as possible. I think she represented everything that I had strived so hard not to become. When I first arrived I had mornings when the effort to face the day was the biggest wrestling match with my soul. It would have been so easy to hide away in bed and not face the raw demons which I contended with each waking moment, but what I discovered was that gradually, as the days wore on, the battle became less fierce and by focusing on positive things like my gymnastics and physical work I was able to heal and grow. I found it simply impossible to even talk to JD; she was incredibly physically weak but she was equally mentally weak and I could not see her surviving let alone thriving.

    What a strain all this was on Adeleine. She had invested so much time and effort into saving JD and now she was going to be disappointed and deflated and possibly put off from reaching out to another poor soul currently imprisoned. I hated to see Adeleine looking sad and after a week of seeing no change in JD and still waiting for Benito to return from Adam's we talked about the situation as we sat on the porch one evening.

"Do you know how long JD was at the dungeon?" I asked Adeleine.

"A bit longer than you I think. I don't know what to do Marna; it was easy with you, you wanted to get on with your life. You had already made a start by improving your physical strength and refusing the dope. In hindsight I should have realised that JD's situation was completely different. Doctor Mahur is very concerned, he's trying to find out whether she has any family. Benito is asking at the bureau as well. A life without hope is no life. You had hope Marna, I see that now. I just assumed she would come here and be delighted to be part of our family and feel accepted and begin to put out her shoots the way you did. Look at these marigolds. I sowed them from seed, at first the tiny shoots look the same but some grow to be strong plants and produce beautiful flowers, some grow but remain spindly and others die. Maybe they don't fight hard enough to drink enough water and think it is easier to give way to the bigger plants and just fade away. I was thinking about this as I planted them out. Out of about a hundred seeds only about ten make it to be strong and beautiful."

"Yes I know what you are saying but I am worried that you will now become disheartened and give up trying to help other girls. There is still time for JD to change and they are not all like her, we cannot give up. I recognise how hard it is and I know you don't have much time to talk to the girls before they have to make the decision to leave with you or not, but I think you could suggest spitting out the drugs and at least doing a few press ups, it would help."

"You are a good girl Marna, it is not fair for you to carry this burden. If I have learnt anything from this experience with JD it is that this problem is an awful lot bigger than any of us envisioned. We are not professionals, I don't know how to motivate JD and get her to have the courage to come out of her room and start eating and begin her healing progress. Even Doctor Mahur is not qualified to counsel these deep rooted, complex issues. I thought it was sufficient to scoop her up, let her enjoy the fresh air and feel the warm sun on her face, feed her my butter muffins and all would be well! How misguided was I? I wish Benito was here but I have a horrible feeling I know what his reaction will be when he returns and I won't blame him."

Benito returned the following day. I overheard enough of their telephone conversation the previous evening to know that he had managed to procure Paul's birth certificate. Was I happy to hear that information? I didn't know whether he had any news about JD's family but there had been so much happening all of a sudden that I felt overwhelmed by it all and I did not really understand why but I had an almost compelling desire to pack my bag and run away.

Mary Daniels

Chapter 31

The fleeting desire passed and I did not run away. I knew I would have to talk with Paul at some point in the near future and I needed to confront a huge amount of matters. When I first arrived at Benito and Adeleine's home they suggested that I have some counselling. Doctor Mahur had spoken to me about it and told me that Benito and Adeleine had made it clear that they were more than willing to pay for me to have any help that Doctor Mahur thought best.

The very fact that these dear, kind hearted people had generously offered to meet all expenses of me having counselling helped me to make the decision that in fact they were all the counselling I needed. To be surrounded by their love and generosity with no mention of a limited length of stay was all that I needed to recover - that and Adeleine's delicious butter muffins of course!

Paul and I spent a couple of pleasant afternoons

Mary Daniels

together; I felt a comforting warmth after I had been with him for any length of time, it was like the welcome warmth of the sun on your face on the first spring day after winter. It wasn't too overpowering, it wouldn't burn you or do any harm, it simply felt agreeable. Is that what it would feel like to be married to Paul I wondered? The very fact that I was questioning it made me sense there were holes in my reasoning - like the sieve that Adeleine used to make fine flour. Holes had uses but not when you wanted to be certain about something!

A few days later I had a visitor, her name was Destiny and how extremely welcome she was! She appeared at the perfect moment. It was when I was weeding the little flower border that went round the porch. I was kneeling back on my heels on my cushion when Benito approached.

"Hey Kipee, that's a grand job you are doing there; I love seeing the bright orange and yellow marigolds, they remind me of the sunshine."

"Yes, it is nice for me and Adeleine to sit on the porch in the evening and look at them. Did you have a nice time with Adam and his family?"

"I did, thank-you, and I have something for you, which is why I came to find you."

And with that he handed me 'my Destiny!' It was a four page leaflet and there was a picture on the front of a young girl swinging high into the crowds of a circus with the words ' flying high' brazened across the top. I opened up the leaflet and read as best as I could as my reading skills were still marginable and I discovered that 'Flying High' was in fact a circus school in the town where Adam lived which is how Benito happened to see it. I understood enough of the text to ascertain that I was suitable for admittance and that the term began in three weeks' time.

The leaflet made it clear that no formal education was necessary and that their priority was flexibility and a motivation to work hard and ultimately join a circus. As I sat on my gardening cushion an unusual thing happened - I felt the sensation of my eyes becoming watery and the words on the leaflet became blurred. Benito looked at me and I saw two, big, shiny streams of tears flowing down his cheeks. We both comprehended this was perfect and words were not necessary but how I longed for my emotions to be liberated as his clearly were. Maybe one day they would be; healing of the soul takes time and I knew that enrolling at Flying High circus school was part of my healing journey.

It never crossed my mind that I would not be accepted into the school. I had unshakable confidence in my gymnastics ability. Even as a young girl I understood that I was a talented gymnast; undoubtedly it helped being double jointed but also I was always flexible - and fearless! That was a huge asset when you are leaping hundreds of feet in the air. I couldn't wait to tell Paul; this was our dream come true. His life would no longer be on hold; he would be near Adam and his nieces and have so many distractions to stop him mulling over his own circumstances constantly. Our married life had to start on a fresh note, we couldn't simply wed and merge into the existence we had been experiencing here; that would not work on so many levels.

And so it was with a lightness of step that I ran across the drive that afternoon as soon as I heard Charmer's approach. He quickly consumed my joy and excitement soon bubbled up through him and he leapt at me so enthusiastically I nearly fell backwards.

"Woah Charmer, careful boy; you nearly knocked Marna over and we don't want that, do we?"

"Indeed we do not." I replied, grinning from ear to ear.

"We can't have me injured or bruised - not when I have an interview to attend."

Well I am not sure how I expected Paul to respond but the silence was deafening and he avoided eye contact by keeping his face firmly looking at the ground like he was searching for a lost pin. I crouched down and hugged Charmer. 'No wonder dogs find it difficult to interpret human behaviour' I thought to myself! Poor Charmer, all he wanted to do was please his master and here he was looking like a lost child when Charmer thought he was in for some excitement.

"I've come to help Benito fix a cabinet for his workshop." Paul informed me.

"I will walk across with you then." I volunteered.

"Aren't you going to ask what my interview is for? I understand you don't like change Paul but sometimes your silence can be infuriating."

I spoke softly and sensitively. Paul reminded me of something I remember doing with Mama. We would carefully make two holes in an egg, one at the top and one at the bottom . Then we would cautiously blow the inside of the egg out and paint the delicate egg shells. It is one of the few memories of Mama which I cling on to and now here was sweet, delicate Paul reminding me of that egg shell. It only took one press of a finger that was slightly too firm and – poof – the egg was shattered.

"I am going to start a course at a circus school in Canuta, you know that is the town where Adam lives. The autumn term starts in three weeks. I can show you the leaflet, Benito heard about it when he stayed with Adam. Please say something Paul, this is the most exciting news I've ever had, please be happy for me."

He nodded, slowly but respectfully. That was one thing I loved about Paul, his gestures and facial expressions spoke a thousand words and I felt as if I knew every single one of them. What he would have said if his years of hurt hadn't swallowed up the words was – "I am incredibly proud of you Marna and so happy for you but I know where this conversation would lead if I had the confidence to engage with you. I do not possess that confidence; I long to be free and fly away with you to Canuto, to share your hopes and aspirations; to be with you when you exceed all your expectations and to be the shoulder that you cry on when things maybe are not how you perceived them to be." These were the words that his poignant nod portrayed. But he knew that if he voiced these words then he would be speaking a desire that had been hidden away inside of him for so long that he wouldn't know where to find it or what to do with that desire if it did happen to find a voice. What I saw when he determinedly kept his head down was one thing and one thing alone - fear. He had managed to survive for many years and on the surface recover from losing his sister but if anything came along to shake that fragile existence he would be in trouble; and that is exactly what had just happened - trouble in the shape of me!

We walked to Benito's workshop side by side with a connection between us that outshone words or touch. I felt so happy to be walking alongside him with dear Charmer bounding joyously behind us, with his tail constantly wagging. I could have asked about the cabinet and Paul would have politely educated me but a) I would not be able to absorb any details and b) I really did not have the energy to try. Benito was waiting for him, building the cabinet was a two man job so I said I would leave them to it. Benito looked at me in such a way that I knew he understood completely what had just happened.

Paul was aware that I had just over two weeks to pack my bags and arrange my journey to Canuto. The circus school had kindly agreed to conduct my interview over the telephone giving the shortness of time before the beginning of term and also the distance from Adeleine's home to Canuto. Adam had kindly said I was welcome to stay with his family - if I didn't mind the chaos! They were his words and I laughed inwardly thinking that could mean a number of things! But one thing that was certain was that it would be fun!

And I am sure that a married life with Paul would have been fun too but he obviously was not ready for any of it. He wasn't willing to even open up a tiny crack for the light of adventure and challenge to seep in - but that was all right. He was being honest and the last thing I wanted was to leave on bad terms and as much as I noticed that he was going out of his way to avoid me I smiled and waved when he walked by. Yes, I still had a flutter inside me when I saw him and I think if I hadn't been so excited about the next step in my life journey I may have felt sad that I would be living far away from him and possibly never see him again.

And so it was that on a bright, late summer morning I set off in a dusty bus for the next chapter of my interesting life. I did not possess enough words to thank Adeleine and Benito for all they had done for me so I simply hugged them and waved from the dirty window of the bus. There were a million emotions swirling around my being but I knew I was about to be Flying High.

The End

Printed in Poland
by Amazon Fulfillment
Poland Sp. z o.o., Wrocław